Critical Acclaim for *Speak English*

Mike Palecek's writing is always a pleasure to sneak off to a quiet place and devour ... Deceivingly simple sentences that are easy on the eyes, yet deep, powerful & enduring on the brain ... haunting "fictional" truths ...

◆ Betsy Metz is an Independent 9/11 Truth Activist

There is more truth in Mike Palecek's books than anyone can find in *The New York Times*.

◆ Jim Fetzer is an American philosopher and professor emeritus at the University of Minnesota Duluth

Mike Palecek has been a consistently good writer about the real America, not the one we pretend we live in.

◆ Meria Heller produces and hosts *The Meria Show*

Mike Palecek takes us on a cultural journey into the hyper-realities of an excited delirium of knowinglessness.

◆ Peter Phillips is a Professor of Sociology ad Sonoma State University and former director of Project Censored

The paranormal meets a rite-of-passage tale in plain, American English, and the Alien Question is answered — or is it? Inside-out, 21st century conspiracy theory gets right in your face — I love it!

◆ Lisa B. Falour is the Pushcart Prize nominee author of *I WAS*

Mike Palecek can take the worst events that happen (terrorist planes crashing on purpose into the Twin Towers on 9/11) and make them hilarious. Well, not the event, but our reaction to it. This book is the scariest yet, we are being invaded by aliens. Again, it is our reaction to the invasion that catches Mike's eye. He'll make you laugh a little and then think about how to be a better human being tomorrow. Thanks Mike.

◆ Jeanne Norris heads the Franklin County chapter of Grandmothers For Peace in New York

Speak English

Other books by Mike Palecek

Fiction:

Killing George Bush, Publish America
Joe Coffee's Revolution, Badger Books
Twins, Badger Books
The Truth, New Hampshire Writers Collective
The Last Liberal Outlaw, New Leaf
Looking For Bigfoot, Howling Dog Press
Terror Nation, Mainstay Press
The American Dream, CWG Press
Iowa Terror, Seventh Street Press
Guests of the Nation, Seventh Street Press
The Progrrressive Avenger, Seventh Street Press

Non-fiction:

Prophets Without Honor, Algora Publishing
    (with William Strabala)
Cost of Freedom, Howling Dog Press
    (one of several writers contributing to this anthology)

Speak English

by Mike Palecek

FIRST EDITION

Published by **CWG Press**,
1204 NE 11th Ave #2,
Fort Lauderdale, FL 33304

978-0-9788186-4-7

5 4 3 2 1

*"We are like butterflies who flutter for a day
and think it's forever."*

— Carl Sagan

[chapter one]

I spent thirty-three years and four
months in active service as a member of
our country's most agile military force
— the Marine Corps.

And during that period I spent most of
my time being a high-class muscle man
for Big Business, for Wall Street and
for the bankers. In short, I was a
racketeer for capitalism.

I suspected I was just part of a racket
all the time.

Now I am sure of it.

    - Maj. General Smedley Butler, USMC,
      1881-1940

"Niggers go long."

Rick falls into the backseat.

A.C. reaches toward the radio.

"No, wait." Rick puts a hand up and pitches
an ear to hear if The Big Red could pull it out
with a Hail Mary.

"Van Brownsen drops back," says the announcer. "He moves left in the pocket. The ball is
up... It's... incomplete."

"Okay. go ahead," he says, waving his hand.

"Shit."

A.C. cuts off the mournful announcers in Lincoln.

"Dream Weaver" buzzes in the dashboard. KSTP, Oklahoma City. Nothing around here except country and polka.

A.C. tunes it.

A little.

Fly me high through the starry skies. Maybe to an astral plane.

It still fuckin' buzzes. It's too early, got to be dark at least, best after midnight.

Rick sticks his face into mine.

Oooo. Clearasil.

"Look at that," I say, looking out my window seeking a new smell.

I down-shift and look.

Out in the stubble a hawk stares at us, daring us to fight, like the boys from Stanton.

Under one foot a rabbit struggles with wide eyes.

It stops and asks us for help.

"Stop!

"Stop!"

Rick puts a hand on my shoulder and one on the shotgun on the floor.

I shrug hard to get his hand off.

I brake, and then go.

Fuckin' Corner.

His brother drowned yesterday.

Fucking yesterday and he's out road huntin' and drinkin'.

Tom Corner was out swimming at the new lake. Brand new lake they made. He was swimming around, out toward the middle. Guess he dived down and some sea weed shit grabbed his ankle and he couldn't get back up.

Makes sense to me. I can see how that could happen.

The whole town was out there watching the fire department in this rowboat, I guess the fire department rowboat.

They gaffed Tom in the thigh and yanked him up into the boat with the coffee thermoses and extra rope.

Blood spreading across the lake.

Rick was there, standing right there with me and A.C., and most of the other guys.

"Kenny," says A.C. "PTTPRO."

Power To The People Right On.

He hands me a fresh can of Schlitz, like some Zen bartender who just knew I needed one. He rolls down his window to toss two cans at a fence post. Left-handed.

The first can hits the top of A.C.'s window, spraying Shits all over the inside of my '57 Chevy.

I swear, holler.

"Oh, shit," said A.C. He apologizes. We dab with hunting jackets, gloves, stocking caps.

He finally nails the fence post. He played baseball up through Babe Ruth League.

I slide it up to second, arranging my hands to steer and drink.

I put my arm in my window and enjoy.

Black and white.

Bench seats, radio works great. All the metal thick, hard, quality. No rust. Everything original, except the tape deck, tires, gas.

A classic and I know it. I knew it the minute I climbed in after my dad brought it home for me. He found it by peeking in some old lady's locked garage.

I tore the mud flaps off and those metal reflectors by the front windows. What are those for?

Every shift, song, or corner turned is a joy in this car. And what's great is that I understand it. Maybe my dad made me understand, but I think I came up with understanding on my own. The mark a great teacher leaves is no mark at all.

They don't make cars like that now.

Ever hear anyone mooning over their old Lumina or Tercel or Accord?

Guys have dreams about these old Chevys, that they wished they had the sense back then to appreciate, same as their first girlfriends.

The Schlitz is not cold. Maybe cool, if you squeeze. A.C.'s got sore knees because he's got the cooler on his side.

Rick's got the guns.

We're all wearing red or blue flannel. And Clearasil.

And the brown canvas hunting jackets are now everywhere. It's hot. Well, not really. It was hot. We walked one field and then we were thirsty and we started drinking. We were going to wait until it got really cold, almost too cold to touch the cans, but we didn't.

When we get up before dawn on a Saturday to go hunting we put on coffee even if we don't drink coffee, or maybe we're hungover, and we put on all these clothes, these big hunting boots when tennis shoes would probably be okay.

And then the guns come up from the basement or out on the porch.

It gives the whole thing gravitas. Well, it does.

And I think our dads think now we're getting down to something serious and we might amount to something. I don't know why they would think that.

For the past few hours we've just been driving around.

We see a bird and we almost stop and jump out to shoot.

For the past hour it's just been Rick shooting out the back window.

There aren't that many pheasants or me and A.C. would be dead by now, from having our ear drums blown out. A big hole in our head from that.

Rick also shoots at squirrels, crows, stop signs.

Poor guy. He just wants to kill something so bad. You can't blame him. But I'm sick of that gun goin' off in the car.

My dad would fucking kill me.

It's fucking loud.

I speed up whenever there's anything running around.

It's like it went off right by your ear.

It's fucking loud.

I turn left to go to Broken Bridge.

By now it was getting almost dark, that's how I remember it.

It's a gravel road, with most of the gravel pushed off toward the sides in a long hump so you have to stay toward the middle, and it's kind of a narrow road anyway.

Broken Bridge is one of the places we would go swimming.

There's a beach, sort of, and in some places the water, it's called Spring Branch Creek or maybe North Fork. The water is deep in some places if you kneel down to piss.

It's mostly a place where you can ask some girls if they want to go out to Broken Bridge or something.

"Party at Broken Bridge," something like that.

It might work.

If it's night, maybe you can bring some beer, but if it's a Sunday it's pretty boring no matter what.

There's rocks on the path, and stickers too, and glass, and most girls know that, so it's not a great place.

The bridge back then was wooden, with high, old iron arcing over the top. It creaked and you could see the water through the cracks in the boards. There was barely room for two cars to pass.

Graffiti decorated the flat iron.

Fuck this. Fuck that. Fuck him. Fuck her.

Way up on the flat angle iron facing southward traffic, way up where someone would really have to want to get up there, in smeared, thick, red, blood, was the legend.

A legend is an old story. It's also an inscription, a title, a motto, or a caption, or an explanation.

It's all of that.

They would have to be shinnying way up and along, hugging with both knees, not looking down. Maybe. Maybe they were the curious type.

Carrying the bloody arm in their teeth.

Then he'd grab the iron with one hand and lean way over to smear the blood words with the arm paintbrush.

There are stories about escaped lunatics.

He'd take it in one hand and write upside down. All those people who write on bridges for cars to see are writing upside down. I'm not sure people understand that. Perhaps it'll just take time.

They said the man who wrote on Broken Bridge was escaped from the state hospital on the other side of town.

He would have strained with all his might and wrapped his legs tight.

And if he was afraid of heights that goes to show how bad he wanted it.

He wrote in big, thick, bloody letters.

I actually visited the state hospital on a Catholic grade school tour once. There were lots of people around, in nurse's uniforms, with droopy eyes and cigarettes hanging on their lips. Industrial women, that's mostly what you get around here.

They had a farm where the inmates could milk. The milk barn was clean and smelled like fresh hay. I remember one guy in there, he was big, with big, really dark black hair.

He picked me out of the group to come over and milk the cow. I didn't want to, but I did it. The girls and everyone else giggled when I grabbed the things.

And if he was escaped, and it was night time, then how did he get out there.

That's a lot of miles on foot, through a xenophobic, nosy town, with nosy, provincial police officers looking for him, who haven't been to college or anywhere, just driving around.

And a lot of those people aren't from around here. How would he know about Broken Bridge anyway.

And to climb in the dark with a bloody arm in his teeth.

Well, he really was into it.

All by himself, a crazy, lonely man in a strange land, playing his crazy game.

With sirens in the distance.

I always wonder if they know they are crazy. Like if a kid with Down's Syndrome knows what he's got. I'm fat. I live on Sixth Street. I'm crazy. Or don't you know?

He's up high on a jagged, rusty piece of iron.

He hears the pitter patter.

He stops. Eyes wide, he looks down and gets
a little dizzy. He grips tighter with his
knees.

His heart pounds.

He bites down on the arm, tastes the blood,
feels the bone, swallows, lets it run down his
chin.

He sees a coyote trotting down the middle of
the bridge.

It trips along kind of sideways, tongue out,
looking about two feet in front.

It passes under him without looking up.

By the light of the orange full moon over
the trees and the river and the retards the
wild man swung down, sweat stinging his eyes
and he wrote.

With all his heart, his soul, he wrote.

He felt those words, dragged them from the
first memories of childhood to that very
moment.

Like Solzhenitsyn, Dickens, Steinbeck,
Faulkner, Dostoyevsky, he wrote.

Behind enemy lines, like King in the
Birmingham jail on used toilet paper.

He wrote.

Fuck You.

[chapter two]

Black & white.
Cute. Little calves.
Tiny front yard fenced.
Little hut.

Big, wide eyes.
Moms moo.
Working class mothers,
In the dairy industry.
Let my children go.

Calf licks the fence.
Metallic, empty.
Women in fur coats
Sit down to eat.

Smiling.
Wipe saliva with blue fingernail.
Still slobber.
Sit. Chat.

Veal is tasty.

— A.T.A.

We headed on toward the bridge.

It was dark by now.

A.C. climbed up into his window and sat on
the ledge, howling, screaming, shit like that.

"Stop," said Rick. "I gotta piss."

I pulled over, leaned forward for him to get
out my side.

A.C. stayed in his window howling.

"Owww!

"Owwwoooo!"

Rick pissed on my back tire. I could see him in my side mirror.

"Hey!"

"What you lookin' at, homo?"

"Owwooo!"

Rick quit pissing on my car.

I snapped off the radio.

A.C. jumped inside.

"Owwoo."

The door opened and Rick pushed me up, then sat down, then he stuck his face up front.

"Owwoooo."

We all opened our eyes wide to listen to this matter-of-fact statement. Kind of in-your-face, sort of. Like a tough guy standing outside the bowling alley on a Friday night, leaning against a dark blue Challenger, a cigarette in one hand, staring down all the jocks as they come out.

Owooo.

A big, white owl swooped right in front of us, turning its head, looking right in at us, its eyes wide and unblinking, probably seeing the same by the dashboard lights, big eyes and mouths, white knuckles on the hard, shined metal.

The owl swooped right straight up about three stories of an elevator shaft to sit on the telephone pole.

We all sat back and breathed.

"Owwooooo!"

This was a low growl, from the woods.

We sat up and jammed our fingertips into the black, shiny, Chevy, metal dashboard.

Something came out from the woods.

You look and you don't know if you are really seeing something.

On our right, next to the river, on the other side of the cut corn.

A shadow tall and straight.

He, it seemed like a he, walked right up to the bridge.

"Put on your lights," A.C. whispered.

I had shut them off for Rick to piss and then he pissed on my car.

Rick pulled away and disappeared into the darkness in back.

I stared straight, squeezed the big wheel with my right hand and reached for the knob with my left.

Rick slammed three shells. You could hear the springs.

I pulled.

I punched the foot button for bright.

We watched it — him — climb the bridge, by hands and by knees, just like in the old story.

Up the side, like a P.E. rope to the ceiling.

Across by two hands, scooch, then grab with the knees.

And then it was like he had just seen our lights and our car. He stood straight up, now with perfect balance.

He howled like Allen Ginsberg.

"Owwoooo!"

He raised his hands over his head and shook them, like a gorilla.

My nose kissed the steering wheel as Rick pushed out.

"Phasers on full-stun," he said.

I honked and it made the guy shake and holler even more.

Rick waved his hand back at me to shut up.

"Let's go!" said A.C., even as he climbed back to sit into his window to get a better look.

"No," I said, low.

I pulled the shifter toward me into first.

A.C. jumped down, then right back up, and popped the top on another, holding it toward the ditch to let the foam run out.

The owl flopped and glided away.

Rick stepped up into the light.

With my toe I punched the lights to dim then back to bright.

We all stared at the guy on the bridge.

Like a skeet shooter Rick put the twelve-gauge to his shoulder and fired.

Boom!

The flash filled the night. A light saber.

The man threw up his arms again, trying to fly on his back.

He fell into the dark.

The boom echoed across the black chill.

I punched the brights off.

We stopped breathing.

Rick's running steps crunched over the gravel.

I smelled powder.

I shot forward. My nose hit the wheel.

The horn blared.

"God!" said A.C., grabbing my shoulder to throw me back.

We sat in silence.

The gunshot echoed around the world and came back.

We breathed.

Hard.

We felt our hearts pound.

We let them pound as much as they wanted.

Well, I floored it.

We skidded out.

I headed straight for the bridge.

"What're you doing!"

Rick screamed and grabbed my shoulders.

I head-butted him backward 'cause I was past sick of that shit. He flew back and we heard pissing and moaning in the back seat.

Apparently he was bleeding.

"What're you doing?" A.C. screamed.

I didn't have time to explain that I couldn't see to turn around and we didn't want to be stuck in the ditch when the police men arrived.

And we didn't want to be heading back toward town to welcome the arriving police men.

The boards buckled as we rolled over the bridge.

A.C. stared into the dark, down over the side of the bridge, at the moon sparkling in the river.

We rattled across, throwing up loose boards.

I punched the lights off.

We hurtled into the night like Apollo in dark space.

Rick and A.C. had a fit.

I lied and told them I could see, barely, by the light of the moon.

I told them we absolutely needed to run silent, deep as a submarine without sound, into the darkest parts of the night we could find, down, down, down.

I had an idea and headed for Stone Road, no relation to A.C.

I turned left and right and right again, onto the lush dark dirt road, more of a path, up a hill, closer to an incline.

The path went on about a mile, maybe less, on a steady rise.

I stopped at the top, next to the little cemetery.

I did a drivers ed. three-point turn-around and we sat there.

The road, or the land, or the cemetery or something belonged to the family of a girl we knew from school — like I say, no relation to ol' A.C.

We often went drinking out here.

You could sit up here and see the lights from town and the highway. You could see the stars and the moon, and sometimes you would get to thinking about things and talking about things you didn't talk about in town.

Deep thoughts.

And you would forget about them just as soon as you turned left off Stone Road toward town and start talking about tits and wieners and football, like the hypnotist at the after-prom party had just snapped his fingers.

And if a car turned onto the road, way down there, you had a long time to get your pants on and climb into the front seat, or to throw the beer into the cemetery.

But you could not escape.

A few times policemen had caught kids up there. I suppose they knew about it and checked it out once in awhile. It's a chance you took.

"It was just a shot in the dark," said A.C.

We were sitting in the pitch black, the quiet, watching a few cars on the highway, probably, oh, two miles away.

"Just a shotgun in pheasant season.

"Nobody's going to care."

"The cops aren't gonna come," said Rick.

He slapped my head pretty hard. I heard him snuffing up blood and snot, so I just rubbed it.

They were right.

"We are in trouble," said A.C.

That was also correct.

"You think?" said Rick.

Through our open windows we smelled manure.

We heard a semi blow its horn a long ways away.

"Shooting star," said Rick.

"Why don't you shoot it," said A.C.

I waited for the "fuck you morphodite asshole bitch" from the back seat black hole. A moo pierced the night and we all jumped. A pasture gate creaked and we looked for the cop lights at the bottom.

"Who was it?" I said, probably not loud enough for anyone to hear.

A.C. turned around.

"Who was it?" he said. "Who did we kill?"

"We?" I asked.

In the mirror I saw Rick looking away, out his window. The moon shined right on him. His eyes were wet looking.

"Alien," he said.

"Riiight," I said.

"What?" A.C. said.

He jumped around to glare at Rick.

"What?"

"A Mexican?" I said.

A.C. said, "Oh, shit."

"A space man," said Rick. "You know." He put his fingers behind his head like *My Favorite Martian* antennas, then let them droop.

"What?" I climbed around onto my knees.

A.C. shoved Rick's shoulder, hard.

"What!"

He shoved him again.

"What!"

Rick pushed A.C. with both hands. A.C. slammed his back on the dashboard and started squealing, trying to reach his back with his hands.

"Fuck off!" said Rick.

"A space man?" I asked. "How do you know? Are you sure? What'd it look like?"

"That's just what it looked like," Rick said. "It just seemed like that. I don't know."

"Then why'd you shoot it?" said A.C. "You idiot."

I shot a look at A.C.

Rick slumped way down in his seat. He was crying hard now.

"We need to go back there," I said as I turned around to stare down the dark road.

"You stupid shit!" said A.C.

"You fuckin' asshole!"

Rick kept crying.

"We need to lose the guns," said A.C.

We sat still for a minute, staring.

The lights of some tiny town were off to the right. I'd never noticed those before. And I think the flashing lights off to the left were from the airport, and then there was the slow moving traffic on the highway, all kind of like a moving painting of night.

And in the foreground...

If you will all just gather around over here, we have the black and white 1957 Chevrolet, with the boys inside who have just murdered an innocent alien being.

And just behind them we have the Stone Family Cemetery, dating back to 1859.

Notice the big moon, the shadows of cows let loose in the cornfield after the harvest.

There's a hint of understated looming gloom, of despair and four lives ended abruptly.

And fathers screaming, mothers crying, grandmothers punching stomachs with both hands.

"Is there a God?" said Rick in a whisper.

"Some people say aliens are God," said A.C.

"Don't say that," I said.

Another shooting star.

"That's the aliens lookin' for their
friend," said A.C.

"Shut up," I said.

And another. Asteroids getting burned up in
our atmosphere.

Or an alien posse, maybe.

It's true that this is an alien hot spot,
for some reason. Lots of people have sightings,
or they say they do.

It could be because there's a regional
collector country school called Area 51. It's
west of town, big playground, really tall
flagpole.

I think kids from three counties go there.

"I think there's a God," I say.

Headlights are coming. It looks like they're
right down on the road.

Oh, shit, we all think.

I start the car.

"Shhh," Rick barks.

If I have to, I'll try to get past it.

That's all I can do, is try.

We'd get caught.

But what else can we do? Sit here and let ourselves be arrested for murder?

"It's not really murder," A.C. says.

The headlights come to the mouth of our road and go past.

"It's an alien. Really."

He turns toward us, pulls his feet up to his chest, presses back against his door.

"Like killing a Mexican."

"Ohhh," Rick groans like he needs to vomit.

"If they don't have papers, it's not like they're real," says A.C.

"Where'd you hear something like that?" I said.

"My dad."

"Your dad," I said at the same time.

"Was he dead?" I turned to ask.

"Blood flew," Rick said. "Every-fucking-where."

"He fell backwards — that's all's I know."

"He might be alive," said A.C.

"We need to go back there," I said.

"It was an alien?" said A.C.

"It had arms," I said.

"And legs," said A.C.

"Aliens have those," said Rick.

"How would you know?" said A.C.

"Cuz I saw them on the guy before I shot him."

"Ohhh," groaned A.C. "That don't make sense."

"Yeah-it-does," said Rick.

I turned around.

"Why did you shoot?"

I turned around more.

"You were going to shoot no matter who it was. Why?"

"No I wasn't."

"You were too," said A.C.

We both stared back into the dark. We couldn't see Rick. Too fucking dark.

"I don't know. I'm sorry. I'm fucking sorry!"

He pounded a fist into the seat and slammed an elbow into the back.

"Shit! God-dammit!"

A.C. and I turned around.

We sat.

We might sit there forever, for a long time.

"What's it feel like?" said A.C., so quiet.

Rick groaned.

"Let me out," he said.

"Let me out!

"Hurry up!"

He fell on his knees, into the ditch.

You could hear him puking.

"If it's an alien, nobody'll ever know," said A.C. while Rick rustled in the weeds like a wounded pheasant.

That's true, I thought.

"How can it be an alien?" I said.

"Maybe it's The Escaped Guy," he said.

"From NFSH," I said.

"I don' know," said A.C.

Rick got in and he smelled like puke.

"Time is it? I got to get home."

"Home?" shouted A.C.

A.C. was right.

We didn't have a home anymore.

No more wars promoted in textbooks.

No more meeting the guys at Arctic Ice every Friday and Saturday night. Maybe sitting in the parking lot all night, or driving around.

You ever wonder why we've got all these military bases overseas?

Nobody wonders. I wonder. The empire.

Ay Yi Yi Yi. I am the Frito Bandito.

Aliens. They would never make a commercial making fun of blacks or Jews or Catholics or Italians. Or Germans for that matter.

I was talking about Area 51 school ya know?

The Walters have this mega Christmas display on their lawn every year, up in the development by the lake. Only rich people celebrate Christmas like that.

Last year somebody put a stuffed alien doll in the sleigh and took Santa out.

No more construction work.

That's a good thing.

We all worked construction in the summer. I tended for some brick layers last year. Rick

worked on a bridge crew, dawn to dusk, for
$2.20 an hour. That's what they paid back then.
Some guys got $1.60. The bricklayers I worked
for got four-something, and I wondered what
they did with all that.

My mom works at HomView Nursing Home. It's
famous, or infamous. We all know we're headed
there.

It smells like urine the minute you step in
the door. Whenever I have to go pick her up I
wait in the parking lot.

She knows I'm out there. She should.

My dad works for Husker Ford.

He's a pretty decent salesman, for all I
know, but he wants to be a writer.

He's got an idea for a whole line of books,
how-to books, explaining to the common guy how
to do things.

How to wire your home, how to learn Spanish,
how to understand economics.

They would all have the same name, the "For
Retards Series."

Spanish For Retards. Electronics For
Retards, like that.

Bob Seger's on the radio, KSTP, clear as a
bell.

He wants to dream like a young man, with the wisdom of an old man.

We live in a newer part of town, on the west side, called Sunset Addition.

Lots of Catholics out there. They're even building a new Catholic Church out there, in addition to the old one downtown.

He wants his home and security. He wants to live like a sailor at sea.

Rick lives way the fuck over on the east side. That's also an addition with a name, Prairie Park.

Lots of young families out there, same as Sunset. The dads in Sunset sell cars and insurance and are in the Knights of Columbus. The dads in Prairie Park work at the steel mill a couple miles away.

A.C. lives in town, in one of the neighborhoods. You think of cities having neighborhoods, turf, well, a town our size does too.

You wouldn't have a clue where they are if you weren't from here, but we know. They aren't drawn out. You don't get beat up for stepping over the line, but you can just kind of feel it.

I don't know. I can't explain it.

The neighborhoods are two, three, four
blocks. Sometimes they have their own
neighborhood grocery store, neighborhood
elementary school, their own legends. Maybe
there's a a famous difficult intersection, or
even their own football and baseball team.
That's if two neighborhoods each have some
organizational genius who has the energy to
call everybody.

In A.C.'s neighborhood they have Hartwig's
Store. In the next neighborhood there's
Braasch's. Hardwood floor, place smells like
cherry popsicles, the people always smile when
you come in like you are some big addition to
their life just by coming in to buy more
baseball cards.

There's also A.C.'s neighborhood, childhood
home of Joe B. Larson, on the west side of the
railroad tracks that eventually run past the
downtown Catholic Church and through the
downtown.

Joe B. Larson is on TV, late night talk
show.

Ten-thirty, that's late for some people.

I'm not sure if it's Joe B. Larson or if
it's just me, but I have this feeling somewhere
inside that the whole world is waiting for
special me. I also have the suspicion that this
feeling is some kind of special psychosis
somewhere in me, waiting, growing, fermenting,

flowering, waiting to bloom just as I step up
to accept my award for Best Man.

Did I mention our family is very Catholic?
There are several breeds of Catholics, like
sheep. Ours is Midwestern Very.

Dad has personal license plates on his new
Ford-something: GOBGRED.

We create enemies because of fear due to
propaganda on purpose.

We had this one nun who taught Religion II
in the high school. She came from China or
Zimbabwe or something. She wasn't white.

Sister Weem-Oh-Way the guys called her.

She said things like that.

That tour of the state hospital we had?

That was in grade school.

Sister Weem-Oh-Way took us out there once
too.

She pointed to each one of those big brick
buildings as our class walked by in front.

World War I, she said, World War II, Korea,
Vietnam.

She said she didn't understand why all those
military bases overseas. And that was thirty-
something years ago or some shit.

An owl hooted.

Maybe it's the same one from the bridge.

We aren't the only murderers in town.

Back in the 1950s or `60s some Negroes from Omaha came through in an Olds — robbed a bank, shot some old people, raped some young women. They were killed in "a hail of bullets" on a side road in Iowa by some of our guys and Iowa farmers in pickups.

Out at Prairie Park some Mexicans just came up to a house on a bright summer Tuesday morning and started screaming.

You know how you can talk loud to make people understand another language? Maybe it was like that.

There were a bunch of women at the house, having their regular young women's Tuesday coffee meeting I think.

And they all got up from their table and started screaming back at these little Mexican men out by the front door.

"Speak English!"

"Speak English!"

"Speak English!"

They screamed and stomped their feet and pulled at their own hair. They might have thrown things.

Maybe the Mexicans wanted directions or
someone was hurt or they needed food or they
had to pee, but they got angry, too. They
rushed the front door and raped all the women
on the kitchen floor.

Then they left, even though they had to pee,
were hungry, and didn't know where they were
going.

The women went back to their coffee and
cookies and cards, and when their husbands all
came home from the steel mill and asked how
their day was, they told them they were all
raped by Mexicans, and they found hamburger at
Safeway for $1.19 for Friday night, and tonight
was going to be TV dinners, chicken, apple
crisp, and mixed vegetables.

And all the men met over at The Lonely Bull,
got to drinkin' and decided to find those
Mexicans. They went drivin' all over three
counties on dirt and gravel roads, shootin'
shotguns out the windows at shadows. And they
never did find them because there never were
Mexicans around here back then.

'Course all these are legends.

It's not possible anymore to tell if they
really happened. But in a way they did happen,
even if they're not real, because people
believe in them, put their trust in them, just
like they believe in Big Red.

You know, you think you know what the world is, that the edge of the world is what you can see in your peripheral vision. That's it.

You think that what you've heard or read or experienced is what there is.

And then when someone shows you a book or information or something that you just had no idea about, you fight it, say that can't be true.

But then you are forced to expand your peripheral vision.

That has happened to me. I think what is wrong with our town is that most people don't get confronted like that, don't come up against this other shit.

"What're we gonna do?" says A.C.

He's slumped down and tired and might be gonna fall asleep.

"The cops are comin' and the aliens are lookin' for us."

Rick still cannot talk without it sounding all whiney and shit. He is turning out to be by far the whiniest murderer that I know.

"We go back, like I said," I said.

[chapter three]

"The pilot, who was not an inhabitant of
this world, was given a Christian burial
in the Aurora Cemetery."

> — Story in the *Fort Worth Register*,
> regarding the alleged crash of an
> extraterrestrial craft in Aurora,
> Texas, 1897. Cited in *Alien Agenda*,
> by Jim Marrs

A.C. has his head all way back and his mouth
open and somethin's gonna land in there. I could
give a shit.

His hat fell outside awhile ago. I'm not
gettin' it.

He's about half bald already. He'd be an old
man by the time he's out of college, but he's
probably not going anyway.

Rick is snoring, stretched out on the back
seat. His legs are curled to his chest 'cause
it's gettin' cold out.

So now I'm all alone and I wonder what we
should do. I watch the bottom road for lights. I
watch so hard I can't see a thing.

You know, they say you shouldn't drink, but
we've actually had some good times out drinking.

There's lots of stories about us.

Legends in our own minds.

I might write a book some day.

One time A.C. and Roy were out riding around with an ear of corn dragging behind their car saying they were out trolling for hogs. That's funny to us.

And Mr. Twede pulled up next to some girls and asked them if they liked eggs then threw an egg that broke on the driver's forehead.

And then everybody was in Mark's dad's pickup, coming back into town from fishing at the sand pit, sitting on folding chairs, drinking quarts of Schlitz, driving down Main. Crosby had a fishing net. A car pulled up alongside and he starts beating on the car with the net. They found out the next day that was Mark's dad's boss.

There's lots more.

None are funny to anyone else.

But to us, we talk about them every time we get together.

Just the mention of Jim holding onto an ice cream cone and that big U-boat steering wheel on the '50 Ford one night, and jamming the ice cream cone into his face as he turned right, sends us flopping on our stomachs.

Or disconnecting Mr. Twede's coil wires, or him driving around Main the whole night with his dome light on.

But everyone got back safe, driving home blind drunk hundreds of times probably, sometimes not remembering the night before.

Well, there were a couple of guys got killed, but only guys we didn't know that good. So they didn't matter. It doesn't take that much to not matter — a couple of blocks, a social class, couple of years.

You only go to the weddings or funerals you can't skip.

There weren't any wars for us. Vietnam ended like the day before we graduated. Some hippie put his head into English class and said, "The war is over!"

We're like, what war?

We would have gone, fought, died, killed, but we never talked about it. That's crazy behavior. I wonder if our whole class was crazy. We talked about sports and girls and drinking.

Nothing about Vietnam. Not Bobby Kennedy. Not Leonard Peltier, nor Fred Hampton or Dan Berrigan. Nobody talked about that stuff — not parents, teachers, priests, ministers, editors, or retards. Nobody.

And if anybody saw any aliens, they sure weren't saying.

And this one girl's dad, out in Sunset, when the Catholic Church started communion in the hand, committed suicide by jumping off the roof of their ranch style home twenty-seven times.

We laughed about that. I wonder if she did. We didn't care. I care now, a little.

Oh, God, they just keep comin'.

One more.

You know how you get those sheets of hundreds of pictures of yourself every year that you are supposed to give out to everyone? One year, somehow, somebody got ahold of Isaac Doherty's pictures. And you would start to see them everywhere. We called them Izzy Doherty handouts.

You'd see a couple in the trophy case, squeezed in between the glass and somehow landing right side up.

And they would be on the bulletin board in the office with the photos of the principal's family, or on Mrs. Gleesen's front desk in English.

I saw one on the bulletin board at Safeway downtown, by the coupons for ice milk — and in the holy water font at church. A.C. said he saw one attached to the ear tag of one of the cows at the auction barn, another inside a plastic menu at Pizza Hut.

Doherty never got mad as far as I know.

That time Weem-Oh-Way took us out to the
state hospital and pointed at the buildings —
remember she said World War I, World War II?

We knew there weren't any soldiers in there,
but nobody wanted to hurt her feelings since
she was from Africa or something. The men
walking around and standing in the windows were
in nightgowns and grotie pajamas, crazy people.

A.C.'s mom used to work out there. I think
she's a nurse or some shit.

That's how he got his nickname. His mom
works a lot, weekends and stuff. Every year
when it was time for his dad to put in the
window air conditioners in the house, A.C. got
roped into helping.

We'd see him up there on a ladder, or
leaning out a window helping his dad. We'd go
by and honk, and you could just see the look on
his face like he had to shit.

One year he came home and he saw the window
units lined up in the driveway. We were going
to play football at Central Park that afternoon
and he decided he wasn't going to miss it.

So he didn't even go inside. He just piled
the air conditioners into his car — front seat,
back seat, trunk — and drove over to the park.

In his mind he said he would just tell his
dad that he was going to do it after the game.
He was just getting all the units together to
get ready to do the job.

We started the game.

We were all sittin' around on the grass, resting, talking about shit, and we see a figure coming across the middle school lawn.

It's wearing a white T-shirt and it's walking tall and straight and fast — straight toward ol' Benedict. When he saw it was his dad he took off running.

His dad ran after him. Benedict ran all the way downtown, through Woolworth's, came out the back and took off for the church.

He hid in one of the confessionals. His dad came into the church and went right for where Benedict was. Drug him out of church and kicked his ass all the way back to the park.

We drove by his house later and there was ol' A.C. up on a ladder, not looking down.

The bridge writer was from there, the state hospital, like I said.

That arm he had?

Nah. I wish I did know where he got it. Nobody knows. Everybody thinks they know, though. If we knew how he got it, whose it was, that would answer a lot of questions.

Actually one question.

There's more.

There's still the overseas bases question, and Big Red. And I wonder why you can't say certain things. And why does KSTP come in only at late night. It does make it cooler, more mysterious that way.

And aliens. There's a question.

And who is the dead guy back in the river?

And what is prison like? What is your whole life in prison like? What is forever and ever in heaven or hell? How can something never stop?

If he even is dead.

I know there was somebody that Rick shot. I saw that part. And I saw him shoot and the guy fall backwards like he was shot.

But I don't know who or what he was.

An alien. Right. That would be better though. We wouldn't get the electric chair for that. Because aliens don't exist.

You can't even talk about them. Not at Thanksgiving Dinner or on the TV news or in the paper or at coffee break. Try doing it once. You can't.

You can't talk about overseas bases at any of those things either, not that anyone does.

And you can't stand up when some important person is talking in an auditorium and ask him what's on your mind.

If you do, somebody will come and smile and show their teeth and take you by the arm. They would end up doing that too, probably, at Thanksgiving Dinner, if you kept it up.

I wonder what "he" was doing howling out there in the night.

And why did he crawl up there, like we were seeing the re-creation of the stump scribbler without the bloody arm?

I think Rick was just scared.

Or maybe he thought for a flash that he would be famous for nailing the Broken Bridge Writer, or maybe he did it because he was sad for his brother, or he might not have thought anything at all. Maybe those kinds just see and shoot.

There weren't any more shooting stars.

No moos.

Or semi's.

No hoo-hooos.

The cemetery was right behind my left shoulder. And there was like some kind of newspaper stuck in one of the evergreen trees and it kept flapping.

I could sort of see the headstones in my rearview mirror, which was pitch black.

I couldn't stop looking.

Rick had stopped snoring.

"Rick."

A.C. was trying to curl up in the front seat.

I put my nose almost to the windshield to see down the road. I saw nothing and every-fucking-thing.

I started the engine and pulled on the lights, carefully.

"I'm going," I said.

I pulled away, slowly, and heard A.C. and Rick moaning and rolling around and hitting their heads, and shit.

I looked straight ahead and behind me and on both sides.

It's like the weeds and trees and barbed wire fence were alive, watching, commenting.

The moon was bright. Not like when there's hard-packed snow everywhere, but pretty light out.

"Roundabout" was on the radio. I forget the band.

I put the clutch in and coasted down.

> Twenty-four-before-my love,
> You'll-see, I'll-be,
> There with you.

When you have participated in the killing of
an alien it sort of shrinks your world, kind of
compresses things, brings everything closer
together.

You kind of look up at the sky like it's
real, there, like the stars and planets are
real.

It used to be like looking up at Christmas
lights all over the sky. Nice, but fakey, not
really real. Not something that affected my
life, more for little kids and shit.

I got down to the bottom and punched on my
brights and then slammed on the brakes.

Shit!

And then I started punching the steering
wheel and silently cursing, whisper-swearing.

Some dumb farmer had put one of those stupid
scarecrows from their front yard right across
from the entrance to Stone Road. Not a
scarecrow, one of those things they make, that
you put different clothes, costumes on, for
different seasons and holidays.

Fucking idiots.

"God-dammit!"

I toed the brights off.

God-damned shit!

Jesus, that scared the shit out of me.

The gravel mumbled under my tires.

I just kept going. Didn't see anybody.

I took a deep breath and turned left onto the dirt road for the bridge.

I could see it up there, all big and wooden and foreboding, like the bridge and moat to a medieval castle. Or, maybe just a really old bridge.

My heart started to pump and pound and I kept going.

I stopped when I got to the bridge because I didn't know what else to do. The moon still shone in the water. Everything was quiet like nothing ever happens around here.

I pulled up slowly onto the wood, over the first board.

Everything bounced and creaked and squeaked and moaned even though I was barely moving.

I kept going.

The slower I went the more noise I made, all creaking and moaning, groaning. Jesus.

The sleeping beauties never woke up.

We passed over the water and I stared down, toward the water, by the water.

I stopped right under where the guy had been standing.

It could have been a girl.

I almost had to puke because of that flash thought of us killing a girl alien. I stuck my head out the window and the cold air helped.

I looked down to where he would have landed on his back. It couldn't have been far from the bridge, maybe in the sand, maybe the water.

I looked for blood, red, green, on the boards or the metal.

I turned off the key. The car relaxed, at-ease.

I thought about it for a second and then I got out.

I stood by the bridge edge and I gulped and looked down, straight into the doe-like dead eyes of Alfred the Alien.

He wasn't there.

I leaned way over.

"Hey."

"Hey!"

"Owwooo."

"Owwwoooo!"

I stood to listen.

Nothing.

"Owwooo, motherfucker."

I shot around and saw A.C. sitting in his window, looking at me over the top of the car.

"What are you *doing*?" he said.

"Shut the fuck up."

"I need to get home," said A.C. "Time is it?"

"Don't know," I lied.

"Where's Rick-dog?"

I pointed to the back seat.

"Sleepin'."

"What're you doing?"

"Whatta you think?"

"Lookin' for the space man?"

"Uh, huh."

I looked back, down into the water, into the woods, to the sky.

"Hey."

I dived inside to the glove compartment at A.C.'s knees and pulled out the flashlight Mom had stashed there for just such situations.

I aimed it into my eyes to test it and blinded myself.

"Niiice." I heard A.C. from the cheap seats.

I moved again to the railing and shined the light at the sand, the water, the trees, gaining confidence, into the sky, way down the river, up at the bridge metal.

I moved around and shined it on the most famous "Fuck You."

"Maybe he flew," said A.C. "No, really.

"He got hit and flew away, like a wounded pheasant. And he got into the trees down the river, buried himself in the dirt to hide, and died, with just his legs sticking out. They can do that."

"Yeah, maybe," I said, still walking my light around.

"What's goin' on?"

Rick's head showed in the back, like a portrait of some kid half drunk waking up in the back seat of a black and white '57 Chevy.

"Hungry," said Rick.

"Paul's," said A.C.

Sometimes after a night of riding around drinking Boone's Farm or Schlitz or Schmidt Big Mouths or Bud Tall Boys we'd go out to Paul's Truck Stop.

It was open all night.

They had Indian waitresses from the south side, and old people who had been out doing old people stuff, and Vietnam Vets who were always there smoking and drinking coffee.

We'd order big meals: biscuits and gravy, hamburgers, fries, pancakes, donuts.

Each guy would eat as fast as he could.

Whoever got done would act like he had to go to the bathroom, maybe say, "I got to go to the bathroom," and then go out the side door and sit in the car.

The last guy at the table was on his own.

Then he comes running and we take off.

"Somebody's coming," A.C. stated.

We looked down the road at the headlights coming our way.

"Get in," Rick told me.

I hurried in as A.C. hopped down from his window seat.

"Go," said Rick. "Ahead."

We moved off slowly toward the lights.

I heard Rick pushing shells into one of the shotguns.

Then six more into another one.

"Gimme one," said A.C.

"What're you doing?" I hollered. I looked at them in the rearview and out the sides of my eyes, keeping my eyes on the lights coming.

Rick passed one of the guns up between the seat and the door.

"Ram 'em," he said.

"What?" I said, keeping my eyes on the bright lights in my face.

"Ram him. We'll kill him and move to Canada."

"Do it," said A.C.

The thing kept coming.

I shifted into second.

Rick and A.C. pumped their guns.

A.C. put a hand on his door handle.

I threw my visor down.

"Jesus!" I said.

I punched my brights.

"Sonsabitch!" said A.C.

"Fucking cops," said Rick.

"Blow him the fuck away," said A.C.

I toed my brights again.

Again.

Again.

I took a deep breath and picked up speed.

Fifteen, twenty.

The whatever dimmed its lights.

I flicked mine down at almost the same time.

We passed.

"No cop," said A.C.

"No shit," I said.

"What was that?" said A.C.

"Mmm,mm," I shrugged.

I drove across town, out on the state hospital road, past the junior college and the state hospital to Prairie Park.

I stopped and Rick shoved me up against the steering wheel.

He loaded his arms with two of the shotguns and the rest of the twelve pack.

He ran around behind and stuck his head in A.C.'s window.

"Don't be saying nothing," he said.

He looked A.C. square in the eyes and then me.

He walked across the grass then turned around.

"It never happened."

[chapter four]

"All right, Beatrice, there was no
alien. The flash of light you saw in the
sky was not a UFO. Swamp gas from a
weather balloon was trapped in a thermal
pocket and reflected the light from
Venus."

"Wait a minute. You just flash that
thing, it erases her memory, and you
just make up a new one?"

"A standard issue neuralyzer."

"And that weak-ass story's the best you
can come up with?"

        — "Men In Black," 1997

"Why the big secret? People are smart.
They can handle it."

"A person is smart. People are dumb,
panicky, dangerous animals and you know
it. Fifteen hundred years ago everybody
knew the Earth was the center of the
universe. Five hundred years ago,
everybody knew the Earth was flat, and
fifteen minutes ago, you knew that
humans were alone on this planet.
Imagine what you'll know tomorrow."

        — "Men In Black"

We all looked out the window at the fields

and farms, cows, some horses, shit like that.

We had not talked to each other for a while. It might have been three solid days we avoided each other. No phone calls, no beers, no eye-contact, no waving on the Main.

But one day I finally couldn't take it anymore. I drove out to pick up Rick. He was standing by his front door. Didn't say a word, just got in and we took off.

We went and got A.C. He was sitting on the roof of his garage. When he sees us he leaps from the roof to this rope his dad has hanging from the tree. It's been there since A.C. was a kid. I wonder how many times he jumped and missed while his dad was yelling at him before he finally got it.

So, A.C. got in and we took off.

I turned left at the gravel road and we saw the bridge.

We kept going.

I pulled right up to it.

We all got out.

We stood right there under the "Fuck You."

"What the fuck is that?" said Rick.

We stepped closer.

Next to the "Fuck You" was a stick drawing of a space man with antennas. Next to him was a space ship, like a state patrolman's hat. Like a cave drawing.

The cave man was pointing to the Fuck You.

"He's telling you 'Fuck You!'" A.C. said loud, laughing.

"Fuck you," said Rick.

"Wow," I said.

Rick just stared up at the hieroglyphics.

A.C. went over to the side to stare.

"I wonder how long that's been there," I said.

"Geezuz, it was an alien," Rick looked at me.

"What?" shouted A.C. "It was?"

"That's what I said," I said. "That's what we said that night."

"We did?" said Rick.

"We did?" A.C. turned toward us.

"See anything?" Rick asked A.C. in a hoarse whisper that meant bones, skin, toes, antennas.

"Aliens," said A.C., looking at the ground then the sky.

"We need to tell someone," said Rick.

I looked at him, stared laser beams.

A.C. wasn't worried. He just wandered over, kicking rocks.

"Nobody'll believe that," he said.

"They have to," said Rick, "it's true."

He pointed at the "Fuck You" on the alien drawing.

He nodded at it, indicating A.C. and me should point at it like some Grange ceremony above the grocery or some shit.

"Oh, brother," I said. Then I pointed.

We used to do stupid shit like this when we stayed out overnight in boxes from the appliance store that we dragged home behind our bikes.

We'd be in somebody's backyard in our white underwear and we might go window peeking or touch each other's dicks or some kind of weird shit.

Oh, brother. It gives me a brain freeze headache to think about that shit.

We would form neighborhood super-hero gangs where we would save everybody for a couple of days. One of them was The Night Watchmen.

I was the biggest boned, so when we'd practice getting onto front porches to save people I would plop down in the flowers on my hands and knees. The other guys would jump on my back and vault onto the porch.

Just then "Rocket Man" began to play on the radio. I must have left the key on.

Which the other guys may or may not have heard, or thought was a sign.

I didn't. Not really.

We need to tell the truth.

The thought occurred to me.

"Let's do something," said Rick.

[chapter five]

UFO probe sought

Believers want to tell their tales to Congress

Friday, May 11, 2001

Las Vegas Review-Journal

WASHINGTON — Donald Phillips insists he saw seven silver objects hover high above an Air Force encampment outside Las Vegas one night in September 1966.

Phillips, a noncommissioned officer at the time, said he was asleep at 1 a.m., when he awoke to hear others talking about objects in the sky. He got up and for 10 minutes watched strange rectangular aircraft dart high overhead. The UFOs would dash across the sky and then come to a sudden halt.

"I thought it was absolutely beautiful," he said. "I think they were communicating with their brotherhood."

He was one of 20 former military or government employees who described their contacts with UFOs at a news conference Wednesday organized by a group called the Disclosure Project.

What we ended up doing was getting on the program for Cultural Awareness Day at HomView Nursing Home.

They had us set up in the cafeteria with a podium.

It smelled like piss and we each took turns speaking.

We had a poster that showed the "Fuck You" and the alien drawing.

We talked about alien sightings over the years, and government cover-ups.

We did a skit, with me in the car and Rick shooting A.C. off the recreation director's desk.

And we closed with some Christmas songs, even though it was summer, because A.C.'s mom said they would like that.

We had cookies and punch afterwards and talked to some old people about how they might have known our grandparents.

A.C. asked one lady if she ever met Christopher Columbus, so Rick hit A.C. hard in the kidney and we had to leave.

A.C. really wanted to know, and his back was killing him. You could tell that. So we went in the Chevy and sat in the parking lot at the old Safeway that is now a hardware store until anyone felt like talking again.

Then we went together to the radio station, and asked a guy from our class who now has the noon talk show if we could be on *Voice of the People*.

He said, "Fuckin-A! Don't tell anyone I said *that*." So one day we were all sitting around this radio booth and taking turns scooting up on our chairs to talk into the microphone.

"So, you say you saw an alien, an extra-terrestrial, out by Broken Bridge."

"Something like that," said A.C.

"Yes, we did," said Rick.

"It was at night. Had you been drinking?"

"Yes, we had. Definitely," said A.C.

"You're still certain though?"

"We are," I said, not certain at all.

"Perhaps you killed a human being that night. Have you considered that?"

"Not really," said A.C. in his most professional radio voice, leaning his head in.

Rick bumped heads with A.C. trying to get to the microphone.

"Fuck-yeah. Every minute, second, of every day," he stated.

"Sorry," I leaned in, grabbing Rick out of the way.

"You can't say fuck," A.C. hissed. "Fu-uck."

"You would then be charged with murder."

"Yes, we would," said A.C., again in his new professional persona.

"If they found a body," I pushed in.

"Have you contacted law enforcement?"

"Not yet," I growled, looking our host square in his smiling eyes.

"We are here to talk about aliens," I said. "There are aliens. We are not alone. We know that. The government is keeping the truth from us. We killed an alien near here. We want the people to know. The aliens have tried communicating with us."

"What did they say?"

"Fuck you," said A.C., pushing to the mic.

"Fuck you," said Rick at the same time.

I nodded, shrugged my shoulders, put my hands up and said, "Fuck you."

After a commercial we spent the last half hour answering questions and comments from callers.

Afterwards we got into the Chevy and drove to the parking lot that used to be the YMCA, to sit and watch people coming into the bank.

[chapter six]

We wrung our bread
From stocks and stones
And fenced our gardens
With the red man's bones.

America was founded by people like Anne
Coulter, Sean Hannity, Rush Limbaugh and
the rest of the ass kicking, head
smashing mafia, who back then called
themselves the Pilgrims. The so-called
Founding Fathers are anomalies in this
sea of bottom feeding human beings. We
are still living today with the
dichotomy — and the Pilgrims are winning
and winning big. Only now, the gardens
are being fenced with the bones of the
poor and the middle class.

> — Comments section, *Common Dreams*
> website

Well, shit.

A.C.'s sign said, "We Shot Peter Allen."

Rick's said, "I Shot The ~~Sheriff~~ Mexican."

Mine said, "Aliens Are Real, People."

We were standing with the signs outside the
post office, on the front walk, across from the
library.

Everybody we had ever known was driving past.

"How long we gonna stand here?" said A.C.

"We just got here," I said.

"This is very cool," said Rick. "How cool is this?"

"Not very," said A.C.

"Rick?" A.C. shouted from his side of the walk. "Would you please shoot me, now?"

Rick showed A.C. the bird behind his sign.

"The secret to life, dude," said A.C. "You've got the gift."

I'm sure people who didn't even have mail were driving through the lane.

Many of them were laughing, pointing, lots of kids.

Kids in cars from the high school when it let out and a bit later, kids from the middle school and elementary started to show up.

Half the time A.C.'s sign was upside-down from him putting it down to light a cigarette.

And Rick had car loads of guys with deep dark hair driving past him slow, and two young boys on bikes were sitting on the terrace in front of him, staring, with their arms crossed.

Rick tried to speak Spanish to them and might have made it worse.

Stuff he had seen on the overhead menu at Taco John's.

The newspaper sent a photographer, who just took our names and ages, didn't really have time for our little bridge story.

The radio sent somebody down, an intern from the community college: Jessica. She listened and smiled and recorded everything we said for about forty-five minutes. A.C. smoked about ten cigarettes telling her about that night, and Rick did the howls and the gunshot.

She put the thin little portable microphone to her mouth.

"Did you ever find an alien body?"

Then she put it back to us and A.C. turned away to smoke.

Rick shouted at the little kids on bikes, something from the dessert category.

"No," I said.

"Then how do you know?" she said. "How do you know aliens are real? Why do you think you shot an alien out at Broken Bridge?"

And then the little microphone was right back at my nose.

And I wondered why the radio station even put us on, and why Jessica was here now, because it would be more efficient to just not let us say anything, not let people hear us.

And I wondered if there was this guy or this woman inside the radio station, somebody in an office, who had also seen the aliens, and who now had a chance to tell the story without getting in trouble.

Or, maybe they just wanted to make fun of us, tell the Halloween alien story for the year.

And by then ol' Jessica was in her car slamming her door shut.

When Jessica left in her Gremlin with the red radio station lettering, a police car came in to the post office lane from the north end.

Another pulled in from the south side.

Then they both turned their lights on, no sirens.

Another cruiser stopped on the street and put its flashers on as well.

Three cops stepped out.

One of the kids on the bikes took off. The other just stared at us and the cops.

We could see state patrol vehicles across in the library lot and A.C. said he heard a black helicopter.

Rick said it was the secret government alien police.

"How do you hear a black helicopter?" I said later.

Later in the holding tank we would argue about whether it was just taking someone to the Omaha hospital from the nursing home.

"Probably some old lady who died from you bringing cooties into the home," A.C. told Rick.

Rick raised his hand like he was going to thump him and A.C. stepped back quick.

[chapter seven]

[ ] said: "A most wonderful history."

Say what??? Which history are you
talking about? The genocide of the
Native Americans? Or is it the slaughter
of Mexicans and expropriation of Mexican
land? Or is it the brutal oppression of
the working class by the elites over 2
1/2 centuries? Or could it be the
senseless and unnecessary nuking of two
Japanese cities. I know, it's the
constant meddling and evil influence the
CIA has had on numerous countries. All
wonderful things.

> — Comments section, *Common Dreams*
>   website

Well, I saw those guys in the '57 Chevy.

Nice ride.

And I saw the one get out and shoot Carl.

Carl was just howling at the moon, that's
what we call it.

He's one of those.

They are a sub-culture on Los Gatos that
might compare to cowboys, our name for
earthlings.

Boy, that threw us for a while, trying to
figure that one out. It took years of research

with human samples and cow samples, trying to figure out the "cow-boy" thing.

We understand now, thanks to drobnya and drobnya of watching Bonanza in the lab.

Very sneaky of yourselves, don't you think? Or maybe it's stupidity. There are two schools of thought on that.

Carl is a "C."

There are also P's, T's, D's, G's, Z's and E's — and of course, A's.

There's Curt, Carla, Cody, Cindy, Cathy, Cerl, Cynthia, Cade, Cid, Cat.

The C's. You get it.

The C's exist on Jello, toast, and bread. And breakfast burritos. They are basically invisible, nobody knows about them — surely no one on earth. They snack too much, come to earth too much, and over the course of a long time they can't seem to live without it.

The snacking and the earth thing. Things. Two separate things.

I drive the Earth-Space Shuttle. It's a regional transit bus. A lot of what we get is C traffic.

They were down here that night for a school reunion at Area 51 Collector School.

I was also their school bus driver. They requested me for the reunion night.

Some of them were drinking.

We were in quiet mode, which means
invisible, I understand, sitting over the
trees.

Carl had to go. He wanted to pee off the
bridge, though we've got facilities on-board of
course.

Anyone would have to wonder about the secret
life of C's.

What they eat. Where they sleep. What they
say.

They are a very interesting group for sure,
perhaps like your own gopher trappers, hunters,
meat choppers.

The C's live in the rural areas mostly.

They are a shade of red, almost maroon.

P's are green, of course. G's are blue, and
A's are white, etc., etc., yadda yadda yadda.

They smoke a lot, almost always.

They drink as much coffee as they have in
the dacha, and then they get headaches for days
until they can get more coffee, and then they
drink it all right away.

They don't drive, don't fly.

They love purple mountains, and majesty, and
fruited plains — but they tell no one.

They are sneaky. They want everyone to think they can't talk, but they just *don't*.

They can.

It's a control thing. Mechanism.

They can be total assholes.

They have nothing to do with our universities or sports teams, local or global.

They don't govern. They don't vote.

They eat gravel.

Not really.

At least I think not really.

That's just what some people say to be mean, because C's are aggravating.

Allen the Alien.

That's my name.

Don't wear it out.

I am an A, one of the A's.

You might be familiar with some of our group who assimilated to earth back in the 1970s with the express purpose of playing baseball.

They brought with them a typical "A" feature, which is mandatory facial hair.

All I can say is that I am just so interested in you.

Probably more than you are.

You look tired.

I saw this one scene, an old country school, in the country. The school was abandoned, as the farmers and farms went away and there were no more children.

There was a stretch limousine in front of the school house.

It was in Chicago Bears colors, bright orange, dark blue, with Bears emblems in the side windows.

There was snow up to the doors.

There was an old camper parked around the school corner, and a house out back, with dead cars in the snowy lawn.

The side yard was filled with farming equipment: plows, blades, rakes. There was a black Scout, maybe from the '80s, with four flat tires, and every window had one bullet hole.

An old Ryder rental truck without markings sat around one corner, as if hiding from the Bears car. Perhaps. That might be excessive personification.

There was a church kitty-corner from the school, and houses on the other two corners of the four-way stop.

Just south of one of the houses was an old white board building that could have been the neighborhood store decades ago.

I got out and stood, invisible, on the front porch, to look in one of the windows.

The building was stacked to the ceiling with beehives — boxes and boxes, as far back into the old store as you could see with the dim light.

There is a story there.

I am just so interested.

I don't want to be a bus driver forever.

Why am I interested in humans?

Well, for one thing, humans have this Jesus story, myth, some say.

And they all believe in it, or at least all of the ones I have studied.

They go to worship Jesus, every week. Some go more times.

And yet, they do not follow this Jesus.

Instead, they do whatever they want.

I find that astounding.

They seem to understand the universal cosmic consciousness, the astral, the ethereal, and

yet they still employ the primitive military
paradigm.

They are trying to understand how technology
interfaces with thought. I think that is sweet,
kind of like watching ants drag a stick into
their hole, knowing they might be able to do
something with this, then scrambling all over,
going bugshit, because now the stick has
blocked up their hole.

To go to earth, I could do identity theft,
or kill somebody, or invent somebody.

St. Francis of the 21st Century.

That is what I would like to be.

This fascination with earth?

It's like the people in England and Brazil
and Japan and Somalia know all about Britney
Spears, and Alex Rodriguez and George Strait —
they're all very aware of American culture.

There is a universal mind, which intersects
with technology. Man is violating this, unaware
or not, I'm not sure.

Some don't: St. Francis, Ghandi, Julia
Child, Pogo, Goober, Philip Berrigan.

I love animals, and I love the poor, like
the C's.

I am very strange. Those were the words of
my parents the moment I was born.

"He *is* very strange," they said together.

"Jinx!"

I think the fact that they said that is very strange, if you ask me. Nobody has asked me yet.

On my death bed I will have cause to remember that I never told my father I loved him, that I left my mother's side as she lay dying, that I left my pregnant wife-to-be to seek glory. That was the reason our first baby was never born.

There's more.

My sister found out about our father's death in the newspaper.

The reason I had so much trouble in jail and prison is because I am gay.

Oh, sweet Zheeschz, that one can't be true.

I'm not gay, not very, not really. Right? That would be like a death sentence. It's the reason for the school shootings on Earth, and most of the suicides. The overwhelming silence on hot summer days in many small Midwest towns.

Well, I'm already dying, right?

And with me will die about nine of the universe's worst personality disorders.

The prisoners, some of them, called me that. Maybe they call everyone that, but it was like

an invisible laser-surgery tool — a zzzle saw —
into my heart. I was like, how do they know
about that stuff?

It put me in deep depression, deeper than
China. Don't go there if you can avoid it.

But if I didn't wonder, why did it hurt me
so much?

If they would have called me green, I
wouldn't have cared. I know I'm not green.

And then, oh, there's so much more. I
trapped those sparrows with mouse traps under
the snow when I was a kid.

Oh, brother, maybe it's better if I just go
away, away.

Well, I think I made my decision one time. I
was observing one time. You can do that about
anytime you want, if you have wings. Well,
wheels, you might say.

Coming to earth might be compared to you
guys going to the zoo. That's kind of rude,
sorry. Maybe like an outing to Canada or the
Great Lakes.

It's a day trip is what it is. Not some
place you would go on vacation, to really get
away.

Anywho.

I saw this guy.

He was like Gandalf coming into this west
Texas highway café.

White hat, flowing white cape.

I could see he was playing his part, and he
was enjoying it. Who knows who he really was,
only he.

And so, remembering him, I decided to do
that — become a peace activist, a JFK
researcher, moon hoax researcher, and BF
enthusiast, a Waco revenger, OKC official story
doubter, 911 Truther.

I took on the background of that character.
I really committed, became my character, with a
history, a present and maybe a future.

"It all begins with JFK, the history of this
great, doomed country in the modern age."

I heard that somewhere and I took it on as
my character's motivation, kept repeating it,
repeating.

To assume a new identity, at least in the
"A's," you have to apply. You go to a meeting,
not unlike your school board or city council.

They ask you why you want to assimilate. Who
do you want to be, where do you want to go, how
long do you want to be gone? Some never come
back, defect.

And then you rub this clear goo, like hair
gel, all over yourself. You slide down this

tube like a long uterus and *wheee!* from here to earth, while sitting on an inner tube. Round and round you go until you splash down, like Apollo, in the gunky sea of human consciousness and history.

No, I'm kidding.

Basically, you just go.

You get a bus ride, or a friend or relative takes you. Or you can fly yourself, and find long-term parking, but that can be expensive.

And there you are.

Some zap down. But those are the Z's.

So.

I went.

I just went.

I said my pooh-poohs, waved to my folks in the front window of the dacha, elevated out of the driveway — we don't have reverse in our vehicles, we are not as indecisive as you — put it in Soar, cranked the tunes and woosh! I was gone, headed for earth, the center of the universe, the United States. Mason City, Iowa, to be exact.

Home of The Music Man.

My parents knew someone.

Well, it's my uncle who knew the guy, who said I could use his shed to store my '56 cherry, REO Speedwagon.

You do have to do a little more than just go.

You have to squeeeze.

Because of you coming down, there is like a ripple effect on everyone else. Your history and all that affects everything else.

It's kind of weird, but to do that — it's like Ellis Island. You have to go to the old Rialto Theater in Mason City, the Port of Entry.

The Big Squeeeze.

Most downtown buildings in a town are connected, some aren't. Some have tiny spaces between them and the next one.

For what reason God knows.

That space whistles in the wind, literally calling to young boys, like the sirens of old tales.

Next to the Rialto is the Mason City World Furniture Mart, also deceased.

You are enticed to sidle sideways all the way to the end. If you don't make it, you die, maybe. Fat kids probably. Tough kids never.

After the movie the whole gang squeeezes through what they call "The Eye of the Camel's Needle" on the way to the Dairy Drip.

You could beat them all by running around, but you would rather die, might as well die. Your life would be over anyway.

And so you step in to squeeeze.

You step sideways, step, step, step.

Your nose scrapes on the bricks or runs right down a bed joint.

Your belly cuts and bleeds.

Your donger as well.

You can only see out your side vision.

It gets really tight about fifty feet down, about halfway of course.

And you are afraid.

Scared to death.

Maybe you're the last one, or maybe there is another guy behind pushing you to go faster, but you can't hear the other guys, and if you get stuck they would have to take down both buildings to get you out.

Or at least one. But they wouldn't even do that.

They would have to leave you, and your parents would be sad, but forced to admit you were a dumb ass.

Not like your brother.

For a while they would try to feed you by having the best throwers heave wads of bread at you, but it would just hit you in the head and fall, and you couldn't get to it, and it would draws bird swooping all around you.

They'd pour water down on your head in one and five gallon buckets from the roof, but you would just end up trying to catch the drips with your tongue and holler up that you just wish they'd let you die instead.

And so they would.

Your parents and little sister would stand at the far end of the squeeeze and stare down at your stuck dead body, and then go home for cake with all the relatives.

And they'd tie a bunch of plastic flowers to the parking meter closest to the opening.

And one or two years later you would be a bone pile almost halfway through — as well as a junior high legend.

A stupid legend.

Once you squeeze, you might go across the alley to the back door of Sue Z's Café — she was a Z, now she runs the café. It's like that intergalactic bar in Star Wars, with greys and reptilians, and D's, P's, E's, everyone in there.

If you have been to earth before, as I had on my bus trips, then, after you squeeeze you

are teleported to your "point of origin" — the
place you had been before. And then you go from
there.

I parked and started to get really nervous,
wishing there was someone there that I knew to
see me off, but there wasn't, just the families
of all the others going away.

I squeeezed and came out the other end, at
the alley.

I want an adventure.

I want to kill the young men who murdered my
acquaintance and my customer.

I want to stab them and skin them and hang
their heads on something sharp and long and
sticking up.

The C's are weird, but they are family.

Not family, yeech, blehhh.

Thhttppt.

I want to make up for not ramming them with
my bus, rather than thinking of my job and my
schedule, my precious routine, my wife and
gzilltefnnig at home.

And I want to see the world.

My wife won't go, and the gz's have other
things they're interested in these days. They
won't even know I'm gone.

The wife has her job.

She works in a dental office. She's a hygienist. She cleans teeth. That's how we met.

I was a seminarian at the time, in the Foo Foo Faith. We got caught playing dental hygienist and seminarian in the dorm and that was pretty much it.

She says if I go kill the young humans they might put me in prison, on the Earth, and I said. Well, I didn't say anything.

What could I say?

She's right.

And I want to be a writer.

We Starlings don't value our writers. We say get a real job.

Starlings, yep a small, annoying black earth bird. The term for a member of the S's, but also the name for our overall species. As Dave Barry says, I am not making this up.

Nobody reads anymore.

I want to write poetry and be published.

An author.

A poet.

I have things on my mind.

[chapter eight]

You can't arrest me, I'm on a book tour.

    — Michael Moore

HELLO. I'm Allen T. Alyan, somebody from Nebraska who now lives in Iowa, who will soon be taking a country drive, a road trip, because our country seems on the verge of something bad.

Really, I'm not trying to get away.

Actually my mother told me once that when they heard The War of the Worlds broadcast on the radio they got in the car and just drove. Just to be going somewhere seemed to help because they were so scared.

They thought it was the end of the world.

This time the fire.

Well, I suppose I'm plenty scared, but I'm trying to run towards the blaze, trying to see what I can do to put it out.

I have written some books during the Bush era. I'm going on a book tour to promote my latest, *Wake The Eff Up From The American Dream*.

Before I leave I'm also going to send a letter along with a tax form with a black Magic

Marker X through it as a protest against George
W. Bush.

My book is a punch in the nose to George W.
Bush and Karl Rove.

Somebody needs to punch those two in the
nose.

They smirk while others die. They are
getting away with murder. They are robbing us
blind.

By sending off this crossed-out tax form and
taking this drive around the country in my '90
brown Honda with the driver's side window and
radio that don't work I'll feel that I'm at
least doing something.

Because.

Can we say it? ... Out loud? ... In
public? ...

Won't people think we're crazy? ... Won't
they roll their eyes? Wouldn't it be easier to
just talk about American Idol? The people on
Fox and the announcers on the radio don't say
this.

They'd say it if it were true. ... Right?

Because.

They — Bush & Co. — did 9/11 themselves.

They killed Paul Wellstone.

They sent the anthrax.

They lied about WMD.

They stole two presidential elections.

They would never have told us about Abu Ghraib.

They have secret torture prisons around the world that we were never meant to find out about.

They spy on us. And not because of "terrorism."

They steal the oil.

They want power. They want to be rich.

They could care less about us, about the soldiers, about the freedom of the Iraqi people.

They snicker about all that in the back rooms.

Sure they do.

And there's more.

Some [many?] of our news media "professionals" are actually professional propaganda ministers for this cabal. Who can fail to wonder about Fox, Tom Brokaw, Rush Limbaugh and Dan Rather, in this regard.

It sure seems that way.

What's that expression about talking and sounding like a duck?

I was in third grade when our principal, Sr. Ellen, walked into the room just after lunch recess and said the president had been shot.

A few years later I went to sleep wondering if Bobby would make it through the night. And of course, they had killed Martin Luther King two months before.

So, well, now I'm 51, and those my age would do anything to really understand what happened during those few minutes after lunch in Dealey Plaza on Nov. 22, 1963.

My kids will grow up wondering what really happened on Sept. 11, 2001.

Perhaps none of us will ever know. They keep the truth locked away, marked to be opened after we are all dead. The rest they strike out with a black Magic Marker.

But the Bush family is in power.

And American oil companies recorded record profits last year.

The world turns.

They want power. They want to be rich.

Human traits, desires.

Quack.

Wake The Eff Up From The American Dream.

You look outside your window, you see robins and squirrels and Snickers wrappers and Labrador poop.

Fair to partly cloudy.

It's all a fairy tale. You are a living character inside of a children's book, with dragons and monsters and evil kings and queens.

How did we come to this?

We have fake history — our junior high and high school history books should be all in italics, presented with a wink by the teacher handing out the textbooks on the first day of school: Remember the Maine, Pearl Harbor, Gulf of Tonkin, Iran-Contra, Waco, OKC, moon landings, Watergate, stolen elections. Not to mention millionaires in Washington D.C. who spend long days agonizing over the lives and living conditions of dump truck drivers and nurses aides.

Right? Sure they do.

But even so, to talk about conspiracy in the United States ... It's like being a person who has spent the day upstairs alone writing poetry, then steps out onto the corner to hand those poems out to passers by.

Because we accepted the Warren Commission, we got the "9/11 What Controlled Demolition

Commission?" and our children will get the "XYZ Non-Investigation By Rich People Covering Up For Other Rich People Leaving The Poor Folks To Drown, Again."

After the Supreme Court stopped the counting of votes...

Stopped the counting of votes.

Stopped the counting of votes.

I sat by the upstairs window and looked out at the robins and the squirrels and the Labradors and thought, of course they killed the Kennedys. They can do whatever they want.

I thought about tossing a concrete block through the military recruiters' offices over in Sioux City, just to put up some kind of resistance against all this.

I even drove over there, about an hour away, to look around the area and see how I might do it and get away.

I asked others to join me. Nobody wanted to.

Then I drank a quart of beer out on the patio and sort of measured in both hands the weight of a concrete block against a piece of paper, and decided to keep writing.

I don't know what good I can do. Maybe I'm just driving around just to be moving because I'm scared.

Kurt Vonnegut once said that an anti-war novel is as likely to stop war as an anti-glacier novel is to stop glaciers.

But you still gotta. You gotta walk out the back door and put yourself up against that ice and push. Set your feet and lean and get your hands cold. Push with all your might, until you've got no push left.

There are many of us who see the murder of the Iraqi people for gold as evil, and who want their children to grow up in a world not perverted by the mind of Karl Rove. Those are also human traits, desires.

You got something better to do?

Join me. I'll be writing a column along the way.

Note to self:
Kill those little bastards.

[chapter nine]

The godmother of your daughter, Shirley
MacLaine, writes in her new book that
you've sighted a UFO over her home in
Washington state, that you found the
encounter extremely moving, that it was
a triangular craft silent and hovering,
that you felt a connection to your heart
and heard direction in your mind.

"Now," Kucininch was asked, "did you see
a UFO?"

"I did," Kucinich said.

> — Tim Russert asking Rep. Dennis
> Kucinich, during Democratic
> presidential debate

HELLO. Tomorrow I give Rosey a hug and drive
away to Kansas City for the first stop on my
book tour, a meeting of the K.C. Drinking
Liberally group.

It's been one hundred years since I really
went out and socialized. I think this trip will
be a learning experience for me.

Just finished updating the itinerary. There
are seventy-eight stops between drinking with
the liberals in Kansas City to drinking with
the liberals in Colorado Springs on July 3.

Got my car worked on, tune-up, oil, two new
tires. Cost about fifteen hundred or so. And

so, of course, this afternoon I'm going back to
the shop because the windshield wiper fluid
still doesn't spray.

And maybe I should have got that driver's
side window and the radio to work. I don't
know, maybe.

I did figure out the iPod, with the help of
my kids. Rosey bought me a map, and Lisa Casey
from All Hat No Cattle and Bart at Bartcop.com
sent me T-shirts.

Most Awesome.

At 51, it's been awhile, almost thirty
years, since I took my last road trip in my
dad's 1959 Chevy with the wings, and my dog,
and the cowboy hat I bought in Fort Collins
after visiting my sister.

I always called her derisively "my rich
sister." I shouldn't have done that.

That's maybe not fair, but her husband, once
the manager of KCOL radio in Fort Collins, was
up on the dais when President Gerald Ford
visited Fort Collins in the 1970s.

I don't like Gerald Ford. Nobody should.
He's dead and I don't like him any better. He
was supposed to be a man's president, football
player and all. If he was half a man he
wouldn't have lied to us all with the rest of
the Warren Commission.

Oh, well, what you gonna do with rich bastards? About all you can do is holler. They're still gonna do whatever it is they do.

Anyway, there I was, in dad's brown and white Chevy, my dog, Nicki, sitting in the front seat, ears flapping in the breeze, looking around at me and out the window with Buddhist detachment.

Headed out west, to Oregon, to find the sun, the truth, the girl of my dreams, my ass with both hands.

I really don't know.

Dad died in 1981 in an Omaha hospital, of kidney failure, the day before Rosey and I got married. That has been awhile, too.

Wish I still had the white plastic Jesus we used to have on the dashboard of the Chevy.

It might come in handy.

I never did want to do this, take a book tour.

In my mind, that's the reason you write books, because you don't or won't talk. But my books are good, really, trust me, and they deserve a chance to live.

So I'm going to give about eighty speeches more than I have ever given in my life — and I think it will be a blast.

When it's all over. After I get back and sit with a quart of beer in both hands on the back porch — that kind of a blast, not necessarily while I'm on the road.

Oh, well, that's enough.

I need to just go do it.

Right. I hear you.

First, I need to put this letter to the IRS in the mail.

Seeya

                — Allen

[chapter ten]

Somewhere, something incredible is
waiting to be known.

— Carl Sagan

OMAHA — It's incredible the number of times I
have to pull over to pee.

I am still trying to get use to using reverse
gear.

So far I have nicked an old lady, freaking
destroyed I don't know how many metal garbage
cans, and smooshed about ninety full cans of
soda. They spray and everything gets sticky. Why
don't they just drink it?

Hello from the road.

The *Wake The Eff Up From The American Dream*
Book Tour & Protest Across the USA has arrived
in Omaha.

This past week I left my home in Sheldon,
Iowa and traveled south to Kansas City, then
Newton, Kansas, Lawrence, then back to Kansas
City, and now Omaha.

I am so lucky to have this chance to see all
this, to meet these people, to try to fight the
murderous Bush government, the killers of Paul
Wellstone, the perpetrators of 9-11 — torturers,
thieves, killers of young people, men, women,
and babies.

All thanks to Rosey for her support and letting me have this unbelievable opportunity. I'm staying this week with Kevin and Laura McGuire.

Rosey and I lived with the McGuires and others during the 1980s in a resistance community in Omaha called Greenfields, which Kevin named after an anti-war song, The Green Fields of France.

Wednesday night I met with the Kansas City Drinking Liberally group in downtown K.C. at Harling's bar, and stayed with someone who writes greeting cards for Hallmark.

Then Thursday, it was on to the Mennonite community of Newton, where I stayed with Don and Eleanor Kaufman. Don is from Rosey's home town of Freeman, South Dakota.

Eleanor is on the board of A Thousand Villages and Don is a tireless, lifelong peacemaker and war tax resister.

I spoke to a group of six at Peace Connections on Main Street in Newton, then down the street to Faith & Life bookstore where I sat through my first-ever book signing, just me and the table.

I did manage to sell one book.

In Lawrence I spoke at the public library on Friday evening, then Saturday joined the weekly anti-war vigil at the courthouse before heading across the street to the Solidarity bookstore

to introduce myself. Met some great people,
notably Marvin, who has just gone through
prostate cancer surgery yet still makes it to
the vigils and also works at the local soup
kitchen.

It was very cool to have Greg and Michelle
Albrecht in Lawrence shooting a documentary of
my book tour. They also met me in Omaha the
week before to film at the Pottawattamie County
Jail, the Douglas County Jail, St. Cecilia's
Cathedral and Offutt Air Force Base.

In Lawrence I stayed with Char and Joe
Grant. Joe's biography is one of the amazing
American resistance stories waiting to be told.

He has tales to tell of the Cuban
revolution, Leavenworth penitentiary and
independent publishing.

He once had his paper in Cedar Rapids burned
down because he was doing his job too well.
Nobody burned down Dan Rather's building. There
would be no need.

In Kansas City, on Saturday night, I spoke
to four people at the Crossroads Infoshop on
Troost Avenue.

Before the talk I drove around the
neighborhood and looked at the murals of Martin
Luther King Jr. I sat in the parking lot at
McDonald's, catching up on my writing and
wondering why the blacks live here, looking
down those streets into those neighborhoods. I

wondered what goes on there, what stories are there that need to be told.

And why is it that black people live in neighborhoods like this. How did that happen and why do we tolerate it?

On the way out of Kansas City that night the highway passed the downtown area and I could see the big buildings and the lights out of the corner of my eye while I clutched the paper with the directions in both hands on the steering wheel.

I remembered coming to Kansas City once in the '80s from Omaha on a bus, walking the streets, "becoming a homeless person on purpose."

I took the bus back to Omaha later that night. I couldn't be a homeless person. I had a place to go to. I couldn't go where I did not belong.

So many smart people I'm meeting.

It reminds me of my first experiences as a peacenik in Saint Paul, Washington, New York, Omaha — everyone so smart.

I shouldn't be here. I hang around anyway.

I am way outside my comfort zone as I drive around these cities and meet and speak to these people. It's good for me, as my comfort zone is sitting on the sofa with a yellow and red afghan pulled over my head.

I did a phone interview on the way to Newton with a reporter from Sioux Falls who agreed with me that Bush and Co. did 9-11 themselves.

That night I was suffering from iPod withdrawal as somehow I lost all 259 songs. I was going down the road without Natalie Maines, John Prine, Guy Clark, Jerry Jeff Walker, Jackson Browne.

I turned on the radio and heard the usual clutter, turned it off and enjoyed being away from America for a while.

When I drive I gawk.

I'm always looking for Bigfoot, not in the metaphorical sense of one of my books, but in da flesh. I think I saw one once near Spearfish, South Dakota in the early '80s, and once on a rainy night on the interstate in southern Minnesota in the early '90s.

I also like to look at old, lonesome dirt roads that I pass. The ones that roll, wind, are rocky or muddy or just go on forever to nowhere or to everywhere.

I like to imagine the mystery of where those roads lead and the interesting people at the end.

I remember when Rosey and I moved to the Sandhills of Nebraska in 1990 so that I could work as a reporter on the *Ainsworth Star-Journal*. I loved the idea that there was so much land and so few people.

I had just gone crazy, insane, clinically depressed during six months in the Council Bluffs county jail for civil disobedience at Offutt AFB. The farther away I was from people the better.

Then the first Gulf war came and I wrote in the newspaper that I did not support the troops. We got threats. My column was cancelled.

I quit the paper and we found our own tiny paper to run in southeast Minnesota.

Being in Kansas made me recall the night I arrived at Leavenworth Penitentiary on a prison bus.

It was a dark and stormy night all right.

The lightning cracked and the front steps looked like a thousand steps straight up to hell.

Later I would walk up those steps as a reporter to interview Leonard Peltier and the steps would not seem so steep.

Roads, streets, steps to nowhere, everywhere, dead ends, new beginnings.

I recommend it.

Note to self:
Remember. Kill those little bastards.

[chapter eleven]

Science is not only compatible with
spirituality; it is a profound source of
spirituality.

    — Carl Sagan

Picture Window View, IOWA — Hello all. I am
home this weekend for Easter, watching the Red
Sox and Rangers on Sunday Night baseball.

I was in Lincoln, Omaha, Wayne, Sioux Falls
since writing last.

Lots of memories in Omaha. Rosey and I lived
there during much of the 1980s in a resistance
community in north Omaha called Greenfields,
named after the anti-war song *The Green Fields
of France*.

Oh how do ya do young Willie McBride.
Do you mind if I sit down here by your
graveside?

I think I carved that into my cell in Terre
Haute Penitentiary while I was there for three
weeks waiting transfer to El Reno, Leavenworth
and La Tuna.

Terre Haute. "Dog-ass Terre Haute" somebody
on the prison bus said as we pulled within
sight.

We had come from Chicago and stopped at
Marion earlier in the day to pick up a couple

of guys bound for Leavenworth after years in lockdown at Marion. Or maybe Marion came after Terre Haute. Not sure that I remember anymore. 'Scuse me.

You get out of the prison bus and you walk up toward the big brick penitentiary, through the guard towers and the shotguns and rifles. And you know that none of it has to do with right and wrong.

It has to do with we are bigger than you and we could give a shit about thou shall not kill and the poor and any of that shit and we will kill you if you get out of line and run toward home and your son and your wife.

And 'scuse me, but that walk up from the prison bus to the big brick walls of Terre Haute Penitentiary is where I formed a good deal of my opinion of America.

Even days and weeks and years spent in hot and cold classrooms, wooden desks and Formica desks, listening to Sister Anita, and Lucy, Monique and Luellan — studying American History and religion and English and hygiene from impressive, hard cover textbooks made in Texas — could not compare.

The guns were pointed at me. My son was sitting at home in Nebraska looking out the window wondering when I was coming home.

America. It is big and it will kill you.

It is mean.

It is rich. It is obnoxious. It is
beautiful.

It has people capable of stopping their car
in rush hour traffic to move a baby bird to the
grass, or of looking the other way for forty
years while people suffer and suffer and
finally die.

America.

A big, red-brick-walled country.

But, shit, the people who will stop in
traffic for the little bird are far and few
between, while the ones who will take money to
build big, red brick walls are lined up from
here to the hardware store.

Anyway ... Omaha.

Dog-ass Omaha.

I went to jail for the first time in Omaha,
along with the second, third, fourth and fifth
times.

I went to seminary from Omaha, too.

Took the bus, Greyhound, from New Field to
meet the bishop.

Then up to Saint Paul where I met Fr. Daniel
Berrigan, a priest who said there were better
things than becoming a priest, such as working
for peace and for justice and the poor, and I
believed him.

I still do.

During the summer I got my teeth cleaned back home in New Field, and I guess I liked clean teeth, so I ended up marrying the dental hygienist. We moved to Omaha and moved into Greenfields.

I wrote a letter to Archbishop Daniel Sheehan asking him what he thought of Offutt Air Force Base, home of the Strategic Air Command, which was responsible for the targeting of all of America's nuclear weapons.

Sheehan said the targeting was cool with him and the Catholic Church.

Threatening all those people with murder was cool, spending all those billions of dollars on weapons and not on the poor people of north Omaha was cool with the bishop and the Catholic Church.

So I made up my own little sign.

It said "The Omaha Catholic Church Supports SAC — Why?"

I picketed outside the bishop's offices on Dodge Street, inside his offices, outside the Masses of the jillion Catholic churches in Omaha. I went on a hunger strike once inside Douglas County Correctional Center to try to get the bishop to say "thou shall not kill."

I once stood in front of the congregation at St. Cecilia's Cathedral while the bishop gave his Easter homily, holding my sign.

I once took sanctuary inside the Cathedral, went there instead of going to federal court for an Offutt protest, again asking, demanding that the bishop say "thou shall not kill." He raised a strong chin, firmly placed his red bishop's cap on his head and smoothed his gold-laced, ankle-length robes and said, of course, he would not.

I decided not to let the FBI take me — they were all around the church — one was posing as a stations-of-the-cross sayer inside the church.

While a friend held a diversionary press conference on the front steps I pulled a sweatshirt hood over my head and threw a black garbage sack over my back and walked out a side door, took out the Cathedral garbage, and hopped into the car my wife had left for me in the parking lot.

Rosey and I and our young son were on the run from the FBI for about two nerve-wracking weeks, staying in the cabin of a sympathetic priest, at the mother house of a local religious order, in a friend's apartment, out at her family's farm in South Dakota.

Then I ended up giving myself up at a press conference, again at the Chancery, the bishop's office, after which my wife and son went home alone.

I went to Douglas County Correctional
Center, where I went crazy, insane, clinically
depressed, from missing my young son... And the
bishop? He went golfing.

Dog-ass Catholic Church.

It is big and it will kill you.

[chapter twelve]

I get mean when I have to pee.

— Allen T. Alyan

HEADED TOWARD ROCHESTER, MN — What if you went underground and nobody came looking for you?

Start thinking of yourself as a big deal and by law of nature you will get a rock handed to you on Christmas morning.

Tuesday I went to Spirit Lake, Iowa for a reading. I was feeling pretty good because I have sold some books thus far on my book tour: one here, two there, sometimes three in one place.

Awesome, to my way of thinking.

Stopped into Hill Avenue Books and began visiting with owner Jodi Debs. She pointed to a stack of books by an author who lives within stone-throwing distance.

"I've sold a thousand copies."

A thousand. A thousand?

Geezuz God, a thousand copies of one book?

That's ... well ... well ... that's a lot.

How's that one copy of my book coming along?
I ask.

Fine, just fine. Still right there, over
there.

I go make a visit to my book, check it out,
leaf through it.

Yep. Looks good.

I set it back, kind of on edge, to make it
stand out from the ones next to it. Marketing.

There was a nice crowd at Hill Avenue that
morning.

It was snowing pretty good outside and five
solid souls came out to hear me, some curious
to come see the author mentioned in a letter to
the editor that morning in the Spirit Lake
Dickenson County News saying that Debs should
not have allowed me to speak at her store
because of my anti-war, anti-Bush views and
books.

They passed the protesting note around the
circle and then asked what I thought.

I thought it was okay that the man sent
this. It's not right to try to limit
discussion, which was what he was trying to do,
and what happens routinely on a national scale
in the United States.

Yes, that is wrong, but for the guy to feel
strongly enough to say what he thought, that

part is fine with me. Lots of people might disagree with you, but only the rare ones step out of line to look you in the eye. You have to respect those folks. Though, this man did not show up at my reading.

And, I do have strong views, I guess. I don't know. I think the things I am saying should be on everyone's mind these days.

In my talks I say that I think Bush & Co. carried out the 9-11 attacks.

I also say that they killed Wellstone. I talk about conspiracy in the United States in the same vein as apple pie, Chevrolet, steroids and home runs.

I can't believe we let them get away with killing the woman at Ruby Ridge or the children at Waco, and I think there is reason to believe the FBI was involved with the bombing of the federal building in Oklahoma City.

I have no idea why.

Maybe they would know.

Did we land on the moon a few times back in the 1960s and never go back? I dunno. Could we really get through the radiation belts? Somehow, I doubt it.

Why were there no stars in the photos. Where did that breeze come from to make that American flag ripple perfectly?

And did you ever see the press conference with Buzz Aldrin, Michael Collins and Neil Armstrong after they were supposed to have landed on the moon? They are morose, certainly not excited.

They look dejected. You can imagine by watching the video that they could be depressed at having to be part of such a thing.

They hardly talk at all, and they just came back from the effing moon?

I would be like, dude, you gotta see this place!

Well, it just makes you wonder.

And you read in the last *Rolling Stone* magazine that E. Howard Hunt says it was LBJ and Hoover who had JFK killed?

And the Canadian filmmaker who found footage of CIA agents in the Ambassador Hotel that night, agents who hated the Kennedys and who would have no reason to be there in support of Bobby Kennedy.

It goes on and on.

Somebody said, maybe it was Stalin — the bigger the lie, the easier it is to get people to believe it. It's just too huge to comprehend.

Maybe.

Who knows? Could be.

Sometimes I wonder.

Is that as close as we're ever going to get?

And if so, when will it ever stop?

Probably not.

And that would be the goal of disinformation, to confuse, to convince the public that the real truth will be impossible to find.

That can't be true. The real truth is there.

If we want it.

Maybe we don't want it.

Warren Commission, Gulf of Tonkin, Pearl Harbor, Iran-Contra, torture, WMD, 9/11 Commission — lies, lies, lies.

Any reason to believe these people? I am open to suggestion.

I'm saying that, though it's hard to imagine, anything is possible in the United States, not only in the little guy makes it big sense, but in the they murder in other countries to bring about their desired ends, why not here sense.

Surely not because they are the good guys.

Can we imagine any scenario where Dick
Cheney or Karl Rove, George Bush or Donald
Rumsfeld would say no to an action because of
it being immoral?

Absolutely not.

The only guideline our appointed leaders
employ is whether a certain action will help
them to maintain power. A search for truth, for
right, for goodness, never enters the
discussion, the equation.

But, even so, along the road, I am finding
out that many liberals, progressives, doubt
that Bush & Co. had anything to do with 9-11.

And I will also often get the question, what
political candidate do you support?

Well, I would support anyone who would get
us out of Iraq immediately, initiate a real
investigation into 9-11, and prosecute Bush,
Cheney, Rove, Rumsfeld, Rice, et al for
unspeakable crimes against humanity.

Onward.

See you in Rochester, Des Moines, Iowa City.

[chapter thirteen]

You open up their hearts, and here's
what you'll find ... some humans ain't
human, some people ain't kind.

— John Prine

DRIVING TO DES MOINES — It's sixty-three
songs from Perfect View, Iowa to Rochester,
Minnesota.

I got my iPod back up and running. I won't
be alone anymore. Got the Dixie Chicks, John
Prine, Guy Clark, Jerry Jeff Walker, Mary-
Chapin Carpenter, John Denver, The Clash, Bill
Hicks, Woody Guthrie, Steve Forbert, Harry
McClintock, all squeezed into the brown Honda.

Austin, Minnesota is thirty-four songs from
Rochester.

It is the home of the Spam Museum. I'm probably in there somewhere, maybe in the hall of
fame with all my emails over the past ten years
trying to hawk my books.

In the early 1990s, we lived in Byron, eight
miles west of Rochester. We owned the tiny
Byron Review, ran it out of the north side of
our home on Byron Avenue.

We scrimped and saved and hustled and fought
with the city council, school board, lumber
yard, elevator, fire department, and won the

newspaper of the year award from the MNA in
1994.

We went out of business later in the year.

Sitting in traffic in Rochester was the
first time I felt kind of vulnerable with my
bumper stickers: 9-11 Was An Inside Job, Jail
Bush, Impeach Bush. Rochester is a conservative
island in Minnesota.

But it wasn't really that. I think I was
just tired, depressed a little from having to
leave home and think of three months ahead of
me on the road, and so maybe I was poking along
a little and getting some looks from my fellow
Americans.

But I've got a license to drive slow — Iowa
plates.

And now I remember how fast people in
southeast Minnesota drive. They are busy
people, getting things done, going places. I
try not to get in the way.

Sitting in heavy traffic on Broadway Avenue
in Rochester I kept an eye on the fat blonde
woman behind me with no neck driving the forest
green Dodge Caravan. Had my hand on the auto-
lock in case she opened her door.

Once when I was a seminarian at the College
of St. Thomas in Saint Paul in 1979 I flipped a
trucker the bird as I drove past him in my 1959
brown and white Chevy.

Just because I thought I could get away with it.

As I sang along with the Eagles I could see a familiar truck getting bigger in the rearview mirror. I had to stop and the trucker pulled up next to me, got out of his truck, came around to my door and pounded on the door and the window, saying somebody should teach me a lesson.

I did learn a lesson.

Don't stop.

Or if you have to stop, keep one eye on the lady in the fur-lined jacket in the side mirror.

When we were in Byron in the early '90s I did a story on the Leonard Peltier case, and interviewed an FBI agent in the Rochester agency.

One of them, David Price, was mentioned in the book *In The Spirit of Crazy Horse*, and had been accused by some in the American Indian Movement of having murdered Anna Mae Aquash.

He wasn't in the office the day I was there, so I did not get to meet him. The other, Don Dealing, did visit with me.

He talked about Peltier, Jack Coler, Ronald Williams, Wounded Knee.

He had been at Wounded Knee as a member of some sort of FBI special forces team. By searching Google for Don Dealing tonight I found that he testified in 2004 in a trial regarding the death of Anna Mae Aquash.

He said he was the first FBI agent on the scene. I don't recall talking to him about that.

In the 2004 testimony he also said that his only knowledge of COINTELPRO is through what he has seen "through media and that sort of a thing." Have you ever met an FBI agent? I have talked to a few, while in custody, as a reporter, and while watching a friend be arrested by a boatload of them once in Omaha.

They don't seem human.

They have a non-terrestrial aura. Stay away from them if you can. Your life will be richer for it.

Anyway, I spoke last night to the southeast Minnesota peacemakers group in Rochester, perhaps the most organized peace group in the continental USA. They have name tags and agendas and motions and seconds, and non-acidic tea.

In my talk I raise the question of whether Senator Paul Wellstone was assassinated by the Bush government.

I really didn't know what to expect in giving the talk in Minnesota. But during and afterwards, some said they agreed, and some thanked me for saying out loud what was on people's minds.

They were not aware of Jim Fetzer's book, *American Assassination*.

And so when someone asked what additional information I had about the Wellstone affair, I told them about the book.

And I said that an electro-magnetic weapon was a possibility, and told how the FBI was on the scene too soon not to have left Minneapolis before the plane crashed. And the fire burned blue-white, which is how an electrical fire burns.

These are things I found out from reading Fetzer's book.

I have to admit, out loud, that a lot of what I say comes not from knowing, but from feeling.

I don't apologize for that.

Although I do believe we discovered aliens and alien craft at Roswell, and that our military has been reverse engineering, learning from them, and that could be what we used against Wellstone.

I don't think there is anything wrong with saying what you feel. I would actually like to have someone show me, to my satisfaction, that

I am wrong about Bush and 9-11, Bush and Wellstone. That would be fine with me.

To have to imagine the alternative, that persons within our own government did these things, is not particularly easy to live with. I would be glad to let it go.

I first found out about Wellstone's death when I turned on my computer that day and went to Common Dreams and there was Wellstone's photo.

I then went over to run on the treadmill at nearby Dordt State College, and the Wellstone news was on the TV in the corner.

A couple of college girls were snickering, implying that he got what he deserved. Gotta love those pro-lifers.

The timing of the death of Wellstone was perfect for the Bush administration. They needed that seat to control the Senate.

Wellstone stood in the way of a lot of things.

Think how excited they would be at about that time, after pulling off 9-11, set up perfectly to run the table, to take over the world. Would people like this let one guy stand in their way after all the work and struggle they had committed to become rich and powerful?

Not likely.

There was an investigation. The National Transportation Safety Board determined that pilot error was responsible for the plane not maintaining adequate air speed, which led to a stall from which they could not recover.

And so we can be certain Wellstone was not murdered, because a commission said he was not.

Well, I don't agree.

I think these things can be rigged: the Warren Commission and the 9-11 commission come to mind.

I just think someone like Wellstone, who had heart, who was twice the man, twice the human being, that George W. Bush is, deserved better. He deserves justice. He deserves a real investigation.

He deserves not to be forgotten.

Note to self:
To-Do.
1) Kill those fucking little bastards.

[chapter fourteen]

Get a knife.
Cut. Chew.
Blood. Just a little.
Chew. Chew.
Mmmm. Good.
That's good. Big smile.
Mmmm. Just right.
Cut. Cut.
Blood.
Gotta love it.

— A.T.A.

MINNEAPOLIS — I got a hug from a black lesbian in Iowa City. She was wearing a black stocking cap and heavy coat and dreadlocks.

It was great. A hug.

Wow.

It probably says a lot about me, the way I describe that event. Sorry.

Or not.

I am from New Field, Nebraska. When I lived in New Field the only blacks were the basketball players for New Field Junior College, and the only housing they could find in town was in the locker rooms of the Catholic elementary.

I guess nobody else would rent to them. I remember seeing them in there, coming in and

out, when we went to the gym for P.E., didn't
think anything of it.

Oh, well.

Cherry, "as in tree", made a comment during
my presentation that she didn't come to a point
in her life where she had to "break up with
America" because of finding out the truth.

She never trusted America. She always knew
what it was about. She did not have to go to
prison. She did not have to wonder after 9-11
whether her government could have done it
themselves.

"I totally believe the conspiracy stuff,"
she said. So do I, and I'm from New Field. I
didn't always know about America. I had to
learn it, along the road, from people like
Cherry, like Dan Berrigan, like Kevin McGuire,
Darrell Rupiper, Jean Petersen.

Yesterday I pulled over at a rest stop 40
miles out of Saint Paul to be a guest on a
radio show with Kevin Barrett in Wisconsin.

It was a nice break in a long drive from
Iowa City to Minneapolis, during which I played
and re-played Lyle Lovett's song "If I Had A
Boat" about twelve times because I like the
line from Tonto. That line makes that song,
gives it heart, gave me some strength for the
road, same as the hug from Cherry.

I read at Magers & Quinn Books in Minneapolis last night, and tonight it will be Magus

Books, then tomorrow morning on to Duluth and Winnipeg.

The College of St. Scholastica booked me at the Holiday Inn in Duluth for tomorrow, so I'm hoping to put my feet up at some point and locate a quart of beer and the Twins game. That's high living to my point of view. I'm from New Field.

Well, I'll take this chance to tell you something about my book, since it has turned into a sunny afternoon, and I have a while until I have to try to find my way over to Dinky Town for my 7 p.m. reading.

Wake The Eff Up From The American Dream is a satirical novel which I wrote last summer each day in my head as I drove from my home in Sheldon, Iowa to my work at a group home in Home, Iowa, about twenty minutes away.

Then I wrote it down on paper when I was supposed to be working, then typed it into the computer when I got home, when I was supposed to be mowing the lawn.

The focal character is Michael M.

M also works at a group home. He wants with all his being to get on the Home Helper Show to get his little house fixed up and make his wife happy — while the world burns.

By accident, M rams his moped into the war memorial in city park and breaks the World War II monument. He is whisked away by helicopter to the local concentration camp and called a terrorist. He is dubbed The Big Evil One.

And other stuff happens. I'll tell you more later, if you want.

My thanks to Holly Hart in Iowa City for organizing the event at the public library. Thanks to Marta Carson for the place to stay. It's this refurbished old church out in Amish country outside of Iowa City.

Remember that old Arlo Guthrie song, *Alice's Restaurant*? Isn't there a church in there somewhere? And Marta was playing an Arlo Guthrie song in the morning.

Far out.

Thanks to Jeff Sarmstrom and his family for coming to Magers & Quinn last night. They really made my day.

I'm staying these couple of days with Ed & Carol Felien in south Minneapolis.

Carol teaches women's studies at a local college and Ed runs an alternative Twin Cities newspaper, *The Pulse*.

He has a Che Guevara mousepad.

Now, why couldn't I find a paper like that to work for when I was running around in a fever to be a real reporter?

Ed doesn't know me, but when I emailed him to ask him for a place to stay, he said yes.

Last night after my reading he had wine and cheese and crackers ready and the three of us watched Amy Goodman interview Noam Chomsky and Howard Zinn on the TV.

Howard Zinn talking sense on the television. That is something I have never-ever before seen in my life. I am from New Field.

I had lunch up in *The Pulse* offices today with Ed and his staff: wonderful, rebellious, talented journalists.

Put these people on the TV, on the *Minneapolis Star-Tribune*, the *Washington Post*, and we won't have to put up with the likes of George W. Bush and Karl Rove. [My dislike for Dan Rather, Tom Brokaw, Peter Jennings seems to have not yet found bottom.]

And somebody — some great, wonderful body — gave me a hug after one of my talks. The sun is out, there are kids running around this shop.

It smells like exotic coffee that I do not yet know how to order. There are two guys next to me playing their daily card game, loving every minute of it.

And now it's time to try to find Magus Books.

You take care. Enjoy the day.

Seeya.

[chapter fifteen]

I'll carry it a step further. We see our
visitors as cartoon characters. They
have cultures, they have societies, they
have families, they have loves, they
have dislikes, they have likes, they can
feel pain, and they can feel fear.

　　— Sgt. Clifford Stone, U.S. Army

WATCHING THE TWINS GAME FROM THE DULUTH
HOLIDAY INN — I could not find a quart of beer
on a Wednesday night in Duluth.

Oh, well.

Coors Light bottles will do in a pinch.

I look out the window and I see this old
port city, with these humongous buildings,
board of trade, hotels, that you just know used
to hold millions of sailors every night,
drinking and shit. Quart bottles, no doubt.

It makes you wish you could go out right
this minute and find a boat to go down to the
bottom of Lake Superior, and have Gordon
Lightfoot feel really bad about it.

Or not.

Hey.

Wow. What a night.

I visited the Duluth Catholic Worker, Loaves
& Fishes. And I am on a Dorothy Day high. What
a group. That was fun.

Michele Naar-Obed was one of those sitting
around the living room.

She told how hard it had been for her to be
away from her family while she served eighteen
months in a federal prison in Florida for
pounding on a nuclear submarine.

Her husband, Greg Boertje-Obed, is due to be
released soon from Sandstone prison for
pounding on a missile silo in North Dakota.

And there were lots of other interesting
people there.

I always just sit and listen after I finish
my thing. There are always lots smarter people
than me around who know lots of stuff.

My mission is to shut the eff up and maybe
learn something.

And this afternoon I read at the College of
St. Scholastica, also in Duluth.

You should have seen the spread they put out
there. Beer on ice, wine on ice, cheese on ice,
crackers and broccoli and carrots on ice. And I
couldn't touch any of it, because I am the
honored guest.

So it goes.

Are you like me and everything reminds you of prison or county jail?

Does the play area at McDonald's freak you out because it's hard plastic like county jail chairs and it feels like you're locked in and those workers behind the counter look like county jail guards?

And they're laughing and pointing at you ... and.

Really? You, too?

And does the College of St. Scholastica remind you of a prison, that stone wall, and how tall it is, and the cut, the outline of the top?

You, too?

Dude.

It's got this front wall, and it reminds me of Stillwater state prison. I was never inside, except as a reporter, but, oh, well. Yes. I can talk about something else.

I was walking around the campus before my talk, and I checked out the chapel, which was awesome.

I could sit in there and think about shit for a long time if I had to, but I was nervous before my talk, so I just peeked inside.

Then I walked by a sign that said "St.
Scholastica Monastery."

I once considered the monastery, in Oregon.
I'm not sure they considered me. They would not
let me keep my dog, so I left.

I think it would be great to pray about a
million hours every day. And I don't know that
I would miss the world too much, except for
sex, and Twins baseball, and beer.

Hey.

You should have seen the lineup card I
picked up at Magers & Quinn books in
Minneapolis.

Upcoming Events: Mike Farrell, Allen T.
Alyan, Ralph Nader.

The events manager told me he had about 175
people for Mike Farrell, had to knock out a
wall to fit everyone in.

There were four people at my event and one
of them was a little girl with her parents. I'm
still calling it four.

Hey. The next night over in Dinky Town, near
the U of M, I did a signing at Magus Books.

It was like being in Diagon Alley. They had
bumper stickers about brooms and witches and

stars and being abducted by Neil Armstrong and Buzz Aldrin.

I saw a plaque for "Best Astrology Store." They had crystals, and books on Wiccans and UFOs and the customers were ordering "oils."

Yeah, sure, that probably means, oh, well, it could just be oils. What do you do with oils?

Write me if you know.

The owner was a Brit. He called Bush a "plunker." I smiled as if I knew what that meant because I was the honored guest author.

I think that means retard-war-criminal. I might need a ruling on that. Write me.

On the way up to Duluth from Minneapolis this morning I passed Sandstone. I remember driving up there in the 1980s from Omaha with Rich Koeppen to visit Kevin McGuire in prison.

And later Mary Felion and I would drive up to Duluth from Omaha on a mission to help Rich.

See ... there was this thing about how three resisters from Omaha, in prison for protests at Offutt Air Force Base, were being held too long, past their sentences.

So, we came up with the idea to "Get Rich Quick."

Meaning we would drive up to Duluth and hold signs outside the prison, where Rich Koeppen

was being held, to try to force the federal
government to release him.

It didn't work. Then we drove to Chicago
where Kevin was being held at Metropolitan
Correctional Center, the federal prison in
downtown Chicago, to try to help him, too.

In the meantime, the feds had released Frank
Cordaro from Marion, before we even got there.
Maybe we scared them with our clever slogan.

Anyway, Kevin wasn't waiting for us. He was
on a hunger strike inside MCC in Chicago, saying
they needed to release him or he would not eat.

He was in the doctor's office in MCC, with
the hack doctor shoving an IV up his arm to
force-feed him, when the order came to cut him
loose.

They let him out the side door.

You ever hear of anyone — by a prisoner in
custody — forcing the Bureau of Prisons to
release him?

I have. Kevin McGuire. He beat them. Unheard
of. Awesome. Kevin is Irish.

Somebody needs to write an Irish drinking
song about the bloody British and the lads and
McGuire forcing the bloody, fooking BOP to cut
him loose.

So. We had a party.

Hey.

Before my thing at St. Scholastica. Did I tell you they had my name on the marquee out in front of the school? They did.

No. I don't think it's that. I don't think I'm a big deal and I get off on seeing my name. Oh, I love to see my name. Dude.

It's just that I know how small of a deal I am, and when I see something like that it knocks my socks off, and I have to smile. What if Rosey could see this.

We'd get a chuckle out of it. Maybe go have a beer somewhere.

Well, then I went and parked, put my bags inside the hall and went to explore, made notes about the college looking like a prison, shit like that, then went behind the monastery and walked up to the trees.

I could imagine going into the woods and never coming out.

I really would. And never come out except for sex, or to drink a lot of beer, or to go to a Twins game. I swear I would.

Hey.

See you tomorrow night in Winnipeg. Canada.

Mondragon Books, 7:30 pm.

I have no idea where it is.

[chapter sixteen]

Dead pigs.
Pink and grey.
At the end of the lane.
More every day.
One frozen leg in the air.
Snow-covered.
Four? Six. Seven.
Blisters.
Bloating. Puss.
Wide eyes.
Wide mouths.
Cold wind whistles.
Pretty pigs.

— A.T.A.

PEMBINA PORT OF ENTRY — Oh, Canada.

I'm back.

Did you even notice I was gone?

I was in Canada from about 3:30 p.m. to about 5:15 p.m. this afternoon.

I was trying to get into Canada to go to my book reading in Winnipeg tonight at Mondragon Books.

They asked me at the window who I was, what kind of books did I write, what I was thinking.

Umm, political fiction. Why?

Then they sent me inside. Park under the

ramp.

Talk to the customs people — no, go over there instead, to the immigration folks.

I can do that. How you doing, eh? How about that Red Green Show, huh? I mean, eh?

You know him? I love that show. I want to move to Canada sometime. You folks seem like nice people.

You count your votes, here, right?

How do you feel about anthrax?

Do you have a passport?

Umm, no, I didn't think you had to. I thought that was next year.

Birth certificate? How do I know you are really an American citizen if all you have is an Iowa driver's license?

Hey. How about those Maple Leafs, huh? You skate? I can't skate. I wish I could skate.

Have you ever been arrested?

But I never learned. Yeah. I guess. Hey, lots of ducks around here, eh? I used to hunt. I don't hunt anymore.

Bet it gets cold up here.

Sit down. There.

Well, I guess you guys are stuck with me
now. I always thought Canada was kind of an
option. You know, go up there and sit in the
park, feed bread crumbs to the moose.

But now it looks like this is kind of it.
Canada kicked me out because I have been to
prison for protesting against the United States
military at Offutt Air Force Base.

I thought they would appreciate something
like that. I thought Canadians were different.

Hmmm.

Well, the young woman immigration officer,
agent, takes my papers, my Iowa driver's
license, back to some room down the immigration
hall and disappears for about half an hour,
while Mom & Pop, headed back to Winnipeg from
the winter in Miama, get high-fives from the
immigration and customs staff. I'm sitting over
in the corner on the Group W bench.

The young woman Canadian person comes back
and tells me to come through the swinging doors
with her and please step into the second open
door on the right.

One, two.

We sit down and she explains that I can pay
$200 to make an application to get considered
to enter Canada. Then the application will be
studied and a determination will be made as to

whether I have been rehabilitated enough to sit in a borrowed rowboat and drink Moosehead Beer.

Then I am escorted out of the building. The young immigration woman keeps my dissolute Iowa driver's license in her hand and tells me where I need to turn around to head back to wherever the hell I came from.

She will only hand me back my license as I pass by her on the sidewalk.

I then drive back the quarter mile or so to the United States immigration complex, a crew whose acquaintance I cannot wait to make.

The American immigration window woman asks me why Canada won't take me.

She directs me to Garage Number Two, where I wait until the door opens and American immigration man motions me inside.

He asks me why Canada won't take me.

Mrs. American Immigration Woman stands close by. They both have on fresh protective gloves, kind of a robins-egg blue.

He asks what air force base I protested at that got me sent to prison. I tell him.

He asks if I have ever been to Fort Benning, the School of the Americas.

I say no, but I would like to go there sometime. Mr. American immigration man, young fat blond boy with crew cut, does not smile.

He is fingering, smelling, the money in my billfold.

He directs me to "the waiting room." I know that's what it is because it says "The Waiting Room" on the door. I can see the chairs inside.

I go sit down in one of the chairs and look toward where Mr. & Mrs. American Immigration Persons are ruffling through my undies and political fiction books.

I can't see them.

Because of the one-way window.

You can't watch them as they search your vehicle.

I can hear slamming and clanking and something like dirty socks being sniffed by a drug-smelling Mrs. Immigration American Woman, and I try not to imagine her walking into The Waiting Room with a smile on her face holding a bag of marijuana.

And then they have me. They can put me in Leavenworth or Butterworth or whatever new below-ground federal prison they have these days, and they never have to hear me talking about how Bush did 9-11 and killed Wellstone, ever again.

The door opens.

Mr. New Immigration Man — the other one must have gone home for the day — says that I'm set to go.

Turn right and head back to wherever the hell you came from.

Can I have the paper from The Country Of Canada that says why I can't come in?

No, we keep that.

I turn right, head back to Grand Forks.

I look at the sheet on my passenger seat that Miss Immigration Canadian Person Woman gave me. It's a list of Canadian Consulates in the United States.

That is where I need to send the $200 to get them to study me to see if I am rehabilitated enough to fish in a decent lake.

I wonder how they would make their determination.

Are you glad you broke the law? Yes.

Do you support the United States? No, not really. We suck.

Our military is a bunch of thugs, paid killers.

No money should go to them.

In fact, I sent in a crossed-out tax form to the IRS in Kansas City before I left home on this book tour.

Well, son, looks like you will never see Thunder Bay — ever, in your lifetime.

I think we are through here. We'll take those flapjacks with us, and the flannel shirt, the cedar logs.

I told the woman with a smile that I was not rehabilitated, while we were sitting inside the second open door on the right.

I thought, being Canadian and all, she would understand what I meant.

I wouldn't even try that line down the road with the Americans.

They'd be like, what? Go Packers.

I really thought Canada would be different.

You know, like another country.

Go Maple Leafs.

[chapter seventeen]

When we Indians kill meat, we eat it all
up.
When we dig roots, we make little holes.
When we build houses, we make little
holes.

When we burn grass for grasshoppers, we
don't ruin things.
We shake down acorns and pine nuts.
We don't chop down the trees.
We only use dead wood.

But the White people plow up the ground,
pull down the trees, kill everything.

The White people pay no attention.

How can the spirit of the earth like the
White man?

Everywhere the White man has touched it,
it is sore.

        — Wintu Woman, 19th Century

UNDISCLOSED LOCATION BETWEEN THE INTERSTATE
& THE WOODS — I made it into Wisconsin this
afternoon.

Slipped across the border in between a Fed
Ex van and a white Ford pickup.

Shhh.

I think there might be Canadians in the
hall.

If I am captured in Wisconsin I suspect I will be sent back to Minnesota — just as I was sent packing from Canada yesterday and deported to North Dakota — then no doubt, back to Iowa, where I will be tortured, without a doubt, by endless hours of being exposed to coffee chatter, country music, nine hours of Rush Limbaugh every day, and no minimum speed limit.

I can't go back to Iowa. I won't.

I won't be taken alive.

Shhhh.

The next time I go back to Iowa, it's for life.

I can't do that kind of time.

Shhh!

Somewhere around two o'clock this afternoon, driving south on Highway 53 out of Duluth, headed for Eau Claire, I saw a bald eagle in the ditch, sitting on a deer carcass.

I hate road kill.

That's one of the worst things about driving so much, seeing all the dead animals.

In Kansas I saw a couple of coyotes.

In Nebraska I saw deer waiting on the shoulder for cars and trucks to jump in front of, just to get it over with.

In Iowa, I saw raccoons getting nudged by cars driven by elderly couples and staring down the white hairs with angry scowls.

Hey.

I was passing through Park Rapids, Minnesota earlier today and I was stopped at a light and looked to my left and saw this very impressive two-story brick firehouse with two equally impressive big, red fire trucks inside, and guys inside walking fast with their heads down.

Okay.

We take fires very seriously.

Why couldn't we also have a big, brick building in every town and big, shiny trucks, and when somebody is lonely, or has to make a choice between working for an asshole boss or facing an angry wife, these guys put on their big, red helmets and slick yellow coats and leap into the truck?

How about if somebody wants to work and has little kids and a wife and is walking to Wisconsin from about a million miles away, just to try to get a little house for the wife and the kids on a school bus route?

Hey.

Here's a little more about my book, *Wake The Eff Up From The American Dream* — the reason I am sitting here in a safe house in Wisconsin, surrounded by resistance fighters smoking thin brown cigarettes, wearing black berets, and sporting Tommy guns over their shoulders, on the lookout for white-haired couples trying to return me to Iowa.

Okay, listen up — sit up straight — there are kind of three layers to why it's called *Wake The Eff Up From The American Dream*.

One: Our history is fake: Gulf of Tonkin, John Kennedy assassination, Robert Kennedy assassination, Martin Luther King Jr. assassination, stolen elections, 9-11, propaganda distributed daily by our mainstream press organizations, etc. etc.

Two: The obscenity of pursuing the American Dream while people all over the world struggle to get enough to eat each day.

Three: The futility of pursuing the American Dream — we work two, three, twelve jobs in order to give our children a "good" life — get up at 5 a.m. to take the kids to daycare, then 4 a.m., then 3:30, and people like the Bush family, and other very, very wealthy people keep moving the carrot further and further out of our reach.

We can never reach it. The game is rigged.

Hey.

I remember sitting in The Waiting Room of the vehicle search garage thing at the Pembina Port of Entry yesterday. The sign on the wall said "Homeland Security — Making the United States and Canada Safer."

Really?

You really think so?

George W. Bush and Karl Rove and Dick Cheney and nine other guys did 9-11.

Immigration Persons — what you need to do is go set up your blockade and sensors and computers and stuff in Karl Rove's driveway.

Stand there with your bulletproof vests and handguns. Don't let him into the country.

Putting up a fence across Mexico or Canada to keep poor people out, or people wanting to go read books in Canada is kind of ... well ... stupid.

Let the poor people in, send fire trucks down there to the Arizona border to get them up here as fast as possible so they can get their kids into school and don't make them walk all the way and have to hide from dumb guys to do it.

And let people read books wherever they want. I don't think that's the problem.

The problem is that George W. Bush, Karl Rove, Dick Cheney and Don Rumsfeld carried out 9-11 themselves and murdered Senator Paul Wellstone in order to start a war and get rich.

Mr. Immigration Man in the big garage thing.

Come over here. Yep. Stand right there.

No. Little bit left.

Stop.

Open the hood and take a look inside.

There's your leak, and those guys didn't sneak in here inside the hubcap of an old Honda Accord.

They were driven in by limousine.

See, there's your problem. Right there. Yep.

American Goober, c'mere. Canadian Goober, c'mere.

See? Right thar. Yyyeepp ...

Hey.

Did I ever tell you about the time I woke up a whole Wisconsin state park because I thought there was a bear eating our Doritos in our campsite, and it was really a raccoon?

People came running from all over the campground carrying torches and axes and shit.

And I had to say, oops, I guess it was a
raccoon.

Really?

I thought I told you about that.

Nah, forget it.

Hey.

See you in Madison, Milwaukee, Chicago.

Note to self:
DON'T FORGET!
Kill those stinking little bastards.

[chapter eighteen]

Sgt. Melvin E. Brown later told members
he helped transport alien bodies from
the crash site to a Roswell hanger. He
described them as smaller than humans
with leathery skin like that of a
reptile.

Mother Superior Mary Bernadette, from
the roof of Roswell's St. Mary's
Hospital, saw a bright light go to earth
north of town and recorded the time as
between 11:00 and 11:30 p.m. July 4, in
a logbook.

Sister Capistrano, a Franciscan nun
standing beside Mother Superior
Bernadette at St. Mary's Hospital, also
saw the object come down.

Frankie Rowe was the teenaged daughter
of Dan Dwyer, a Roswell fireman who went
to the scene on Saturday morning and
later told his family he saw the
wreckage of a flying craft, two small
dead bodies, and 'a very small being
about the size of a ten-year-old child.'
According to Rowe, military authorities
threatened her family, and one man told
her if she ever talked about the
incident, she would disappear into the
desert and never be seen again.

     - *Alien Agenda*, by Jim Marrs

THE GRANDVIEW INN — The Boston Red Sox hit
four home runs in one inning tonight against
the New York Yankees.

Ho hum.

George Bush Sr. was involved in the murder
of John F. Kennedy, the Iran-Contra scandal,
stealing two elections for his son, planning
the attacks of 9-11, and on, and on.

Ho hum.

I guess it just all depends.

Well, I'm sitting in the GrandView Inn somewhere on I-94 with my car headed toward
Chicago.

The sign says I am in Racine. I think they
mean "racing".

All I see is The Ramada, Holiday Inn, a
truck parking lot and well, cars, roads, gas
pumps, big signs, people trying with all their
heart and soul to get from wherever they are to
somewhere else.

I got stood up tonight in Milwaukee.

I had a date at the Cream City Collective,
supposed to read there, and nobody, not even
somebody to open the door, shows up.

Being a big-shot author, well, it's not
that.

I mean, I'm this anti-war novelist author guy and here is this anti-war bookstore, with a vegetarian co-op food natural grind, pick and haul your own beans with your own donkey coffee thing across the street, and still I can't get somebody to come open the door.

I drove over here from Madison this afternoon.

I read in Madison yesterday afternoon at a bookstore near the University of Wisconsin.

Beforehand, I was lost, of course, and as an absolute last resort decided to ask for directions.

I pulled into this big lot and drove up to this guy wearing an orange vest.

"Mulch?" he asked.

No, no effing mulch.

Where in the eff is Gilman Street?

He gave me directions, expertly, politely, as only a Madison resident could do.

After my reading, no, before, I go out walking around the "Designated Funk Area."

And it's EarthFest Day Thing, of course.

Every day is effing earth day in Madison.

There is a band up on this stage and, well, they all look like me, like they've been standing up there a long time.

I walk around and there are tables set up for fair trade coffee.

"You like solar energy?" someone asks.

Love it, just love it.

Fair trade coffee, sustainable agriculture, homemade shit of every phylum and fauna, and breasts. Every-effing-where.

The whole thing was put on, evidently, by WISPIRG. I know what that is, do you?

And, I'm walking around and people are laughing at me, gut laughs, some smiles.

It's my all-time best T-shirt ever that Bartcop.com sent to me for this tour.

It has an image of a scowling George W. Bush: Worst President Ever.

It is the best T-shirt ever. I can tell that. I know what is a winner and what isn't. This T-shirt is a winner.

Well, I read to eight people. That's not a bad crowd for me.

I thought I was going to get skunked because at 2 p.m., when it was supposed to start, there were a bunch of chairs, but nobody to sit in them.

The way my "events" go is that I do my thing, my speech, which lasts about thirty minutes, then somebody asks me a question and I

don't know the answer, so the people start
discussing among themselves, which is fine with
me. The people who come to hear me, even though
there are not millions of them, are very smart.
I've noticed that.

And after I speak, they often want the
author to be The Author.

They might ask me, where do you think our
country is, as far as on the path toward
fascism?

And I laugh silently to myself because I
know that I have no effing idea, and then I try
to get them to talk about it amongst
themselves, because I also know that's what
they really want to do anyway.

See, if they came to see a real smart guy
author man person like Ralph Nader, well, he
would have shit to say, about every-effing-
thing, and they could sit there and just
listen.

With me, at my "author events," after I give
my prepared speech, that's kind of it, show's
over, anywhere a guy can find a quart of Old
Style around here?

I'm okay with that.

I know what I know, and I know there is a
definite limit to that, and so I stand in front
of the group and let them talk about paradigms
and para nickels as much as they want, and I
pay attention as long as I can, until my mind

starts wandering, wondering if that was a Kwik
Trip I saw over on Einstein Circle.

After my talk at Rainbow Books in Madison at
2:10 pm., I got directions from Allen Ruff, the
events coordinator, raced to find a place to
stay, made four trips to the ice machine to
cool down the remainder of my twelve pack from
Grand Forks in the sink, rode the exercise
bike, took a shower, then got directions from
the person at the front desk who said she loved
my T-shirt [Dude, I told you], back to the
university area, cursed the low sun, and
sweated myself into finding a parking garage
with some room, then walked with my head down
and my chunky legs just a churnin' over to hear
William Rodgriguez in the Humanities Building.

Rodgriguez was a janitor in the World Trade
Center when 9-11 happened. He was pulled from
the effing rubble.

He is a very good speaker. And he admits
that he looks and sounds like Ricky Ricardo,
which he does.

He helped to save a bunch of people and he
says he heard explosions in the basement before
the planes hit, saw the vending machine guy
walking out of that area with his skin hanging
off his arms from the explosions — before the
planes hit.

He conjectures that the planners didn't
quite coordinate everything — the charges
planted in the buildings and the planes hitting
— exactly together.

He recently visited Venezuela, and was approached by an FBI agent in the hotel.

The Venezuelan government then assigned five men to protect Rodriguez because they thought it just might be possible that the USA would kill Rodriguez in order to silence him, while in the meantime blaming it on Venezuela and giving the land of the free an excuse to invade and silence Chavez, who thinks Bush is the devil, which he is.

[chapter nineteen]

When it comes time to die, be not like
those whose hearts are filled with the
fear of death, so when their time comes
they weep and pray for a little more
time to live their lives over again in a
different way. Sing your death song, and
die like a hero going home.

    - Chief Aupumut, Mohican, 1725

HILLSDALE, MICHIGAN, U.S.A — "I was either
going to fucking move or fucking change this
town." That is Richard Wunsch, the owner of
Volume One Books of Hillsdale, Michigan. "And I
haven't done either."

But he keeps trying.

Geezuz, that means ... everything. That's
the kind of bookstore owners I want in my town.
What if the Ben Franklin Store owner talked
like that, or the Family Table owner, or the
Cenex owner? Living in America wouldn't be so
fucking terrible.

Wunsch has been a first and second grade
teacher in Chicago. He has been a block layer,
a factory worker.

He is a radical, a member of the
intelligentsia of the United States. There
definitely is such a thing.

I am finding that out.

Wunsch is wearing a union jacket while he sits in his bookstore and visits with me and Aimee England — who "runs everything" at the store — as well as visitors strolling in and out of the busy place in downtown Hillsdale, in southern Michigan.

Wunsch talks Steven into sticking around and hearing the rest of my talk. Steven is a young comic, musician, writer.

He works at a grocery store right now. He is an "Army brat," raised in Hawaii, Germany, etc. He has a wife.

He is concerned about the world, aware. He bought a book. And there was this young man over in Chicago, who stopped by to listen to me at Revolution Books. He is from Florida, graduated from high school eight months ago, came to Chicago, by himself, to be an actor.

He asked me what I think about global warming.

These guys have guts, creativity, heart.

I'm not shitting you, it is my absolute pleasure to be able to meet people like this. Wow.

I have met a lot of people like this in the month I have been on the road. Anthony Rayson, also in Chicago, Lou Downey, Michael Stanek, and on and on.

"Chicago Jim" from Bartcop.com stopped by at Barbara's Books and gave me a care package for my journey. How great was that? That gesture is going to take me about four states just on its own.

I probably won't even use any gas.

Many folks are concerned about what is going on in this country. Sometimes they are in the city, some are in the smaller towns.

They are smart, passionate, good people.

And when this war ends, when George W. Bush, Dick Cheney and Karl Rove are run out of the White House with a switch, it will be these people who will have done a good share of the workload. Most of us won't never-ever know them, but they are there, they dare, and they care.

I spent Monday and Tuesday in Chicago with Mike & Audrey Stanek.

Mike took me out bike riding around town. I have not been on a bicycle since, well ... a long time. We took the Blue Line downtown, too.

Mike accompanied me at my readings at New World Resource Center, the Unitarian Church in Park Forest, Revolution Books, Barbara's Books.

Thank you, Mike.

When Mike and I were walking around downtown I could not help but look for Gwen.

She lives in Chicago, I think. She was my first girlfriend in ninth grade in New Field.

We would walk home together and talk and really, the rest of the world did not exist. And now you don't even know where the other one is. How does that happen?

Oh, well, that's kind of how it goes. Kind of how it's supposed to go.

I understand.

Of course I love my wife Rosey. She is my life.

But still I think it is not extraordinary to walk around and wonder where Gwen from 1968 is, and how she is doing.

If that's wrong, I'm sorry. No I'm not.

After the reading Tuesday night at Barbara's, Mike and a friend of his, Carey, from the housing co-op, went for beers and fries and Gouda [it's cheese!] at the Handlebar on North Avenue, an extremist biker bar.

Carey used to work for Greenpeace.

Get this, once during a Chicago peace rally, he was watching a local television station reporter, well, reporting, on the peace protest.

Behind the reporter were some "drunk obnoxious protesters."

After the shot, the reporter turned to "the protesters" and said, "thanks, guys." And the "protesters" walked away, drunk no longer.

Welcome to America, let me try to explain.

Carey has met Julia Hill Butterfly person woman and also Bonnie Raitt, and that's pretty much hugetime in my book.

He had a great suggestion when the inevitable "well what do we do then?" question came up at Barbara's.

Carey said we should write to Rep. John Conyers and demand that these thugs — Bush, Cheney, Rove — be prosecuted before the clock runs out.

These men should be in the super-max prisons we have prepared so judiciously.

Most of the people we have in those tombs do not belong there, because this country is insane — but Bush, Cheney and Rove ... well, it was for these boys that thumb screws were ever even thunk of.

They are murderers.

Mike Stanek, who once spent six months at Indiana's hideous Terre Haute prison for protesting against the U.S. military, also let me download about two hundred new songs onto my iPod and sent me on my way with a brown bag full of Czech beer, from the home country.

What's the word for awesome in Czech?

Nope, I don't know either.

[chapter twenty]

Trucks on the highway.
Tires squealing.
Stacked with turkeys
Crammed in cages.

Trucker stops for coffee.
A thousand eyes follow
Screaming for mercy.

He comes out does not see.
Anything.

How does he drive?

      — A.T.A.

CHICAGO — As we all sat inside Chicago's
Revolution Books waiting to get started,
someone came in and said that local law
enforcement had just conducted a raid in the
heart of the Hispanic community, and that local
residents had responded immediately with a
march in protest.

A front-page photo appeared the next morning
in the *Sun-Times*.

And so I guess that tells us a little about
why and how.

Why don't people get too excited about the
war in Iraq? And how do we mobilize people, get
them in the streets, bring about a non-violent
revolution, as someone in Madison, Wisconsin
suggested?

I think it happens when we feel it affects us. When the city council tries to make us put in a sidewalk in front of our house, then we attend the meeting that night.

The folks in Chicago came out, into the street, immediately, without a mailing list, no matter what was on TV, no matter what plans they had for the evening.

Because the robo cops with the machine guns and the face shields were coming after them. They had to fight. They did not have a choice to make as to whether their time was better spent going out to eat or working in the garden, or whether to fight the brown shirts on their doorstep. There was no decision to make.

From what I have seen I think that's the only way it happens.

Hey.

I just saw that Rosie O'Donnell is off *The View*.

Wow. That tell you anything?

It tells me that George W. Bush and Dick Cheney attacked their own country in order to start the war in Iraq and steal the oil.

Dick Gregory once said in Omaha, somewhere in the mid-1980s, that if you challenge them, "They will bring tanks on your ass."

When I first heard that, in about 1984, I didn't really understand what he was saying, or believe it was that bad in the United States.

It *is* that bad.

It's probably worse.

Hey.

You ever try to find a public restroom in Chicago while you are trying to get out of the city to make it to a book reading in Michigan, and you really, really have to go?

Do you know what happens, eventually?

No, I don't want to talk about it. Would you? If you were a big-time anti-war novelist on a nationwide book tour?

Well, what should we do?

Piss our pants or piss all over the floorboard in fear of the thugs in the police uniforms and government offices?

Or get out in the streets with our signs and our fists in the air?

[chapter twenty-one]

What I'm trying to tell you is that we
are immersed in a universe that is
conscious ... teeming with conscious
intelligence. And there are planets out
there like grains of sand, filled with
intelligent life. And there are
cultures, civilizations, societies ...
that are a million years ahead of us.

> — Retired Command Sergeant Major
>   Robert Dean

SWEETWATERS COFFEE SHOP THING, ANN ARBOR —
Indiana license plates have American flags and
"In God We Trust." Indiana also has more war
memorials per square foot than any other state
in the union. There is also Purple Heart
Highway and Pearl Harbor Memorial Highway and
probably twelve other war highways.

In downtown Indianapolis there is this huge
statue memorial: The Soldiers & Sailors Statue
in The Circle. I know because I was there,
driving nine times around the circle trying to
find my way north on West Street to find
Spencer's Bar to meet with the Indianapolis
Drinking Liberally group.

Meridian — Right.
Right on South.
Left on West.
McCarty to Delaware, left.
Left on East.

Right on Washington.
You can't miss it.

Please don't say that.

Some Indianans most likely believe that
their license plates and the war memorials and
church on Sunday and Jesus are somehow
connected.

Just like some folks believe we landed on
the moon and Osama bin Laden made money on put
options prior to 9-11, like the guy in
Spencer's who gave me directions back to my
hotel.

After leaving Spencer's and heading straight
on McCarty I stopped at a red light and could
see the construction zone for the new stadium
for the Indianapolis Colts. There were lights
all over and cranes and partial walls. It
looked like a set from "Waterworld."

It's supposed to bring a lot of business to
Spencer's after it's completed.

Well, I have been to Indianapolis and
Saginaw, now waiting to go over to The Planet
bookstore on North Main Street in Ann Arbor,
then it's over to Detroit [Oakland County] for
another round of Drinking Liberally.

Rosey called me just as I arrived in
Indianapolis, worried after hearing about an
accident near South Bend that killed eight
people.

"You're not mad about the Days Inn?"

No.

I've been spending a lot of money on motels and gas. About half my stash is already gone.

Anyway.

I had a bad time in Indianapolis.

My own fault.

I drank almost all of Mike Stanek's Czech dark beer gift in one night in Hillsdale, Michigan.

I don't really need to go back to Indianapolis again. Not in this lifetime. Is there a next lifetime? Sometimes I wonder.

You wonder about that?

The sun is out.

It's been rainy lately.

I peed forty-nine times yesterday. Rosey thinks maybe there's something wrong. You think?

But not once in the car. It was a good day.

In fact yesterday was a great day.

I found Saginaw, found The Dawn of a New Day coffee shop and met Ellen, Dawn and Cliff.

Cliff pulled his Michigan map out of his pocket.

He showed me exactly where I was, where Bay City is, Ann Arbor and the UP.

He showed me where Traverse City is, where he went looking for Bigfoot in the 1970s and found a print.

I also talked about Bigfoot with someone at my signing that evening at Barnes & Noble. I must be getting close to my people.

I really got to sit near the front door of a B&N, at a table, with my books, and a poster saying the author was in the store signing copies of *Wake The Eff Up From The American Dream*.

I was sitting there for a while when this little girl walks right up to me, looks me in the eyes and says, "I'm a published author, too."

Awesome. What is your name?

"Delaney."

What is your book about?

"My cat."

Are you writing another book?

"Yes, about my other cat."

Very cool person this Delaney.

After that I read at the 303 Collective, a progressive visual and performing arts space in Old Town, Saginaw.

I walked in and it was kind of dark, candles every-effing-where, and somebody up on stage reading poetry — and there were people in the seats.

Afterward I met lots of great people, some fellow 9-11 Truthers, lots of young people. They shook my hand and smiled and that means a lot, just like meeting Delaney.

The 303 Collective — and particularly this talented guy named Marc Beaudin — is a bunch of people doing original, creative, timely art.

It is great.

Marc says there are groups doing this kind of work in Minneapolis and elsewhere, but I'm just really impressed.

I guess the main thing is that it is original. These people really are putting themselves into this work, shaping their lives around their art, trying to make a difference, and actually doing it.

Hey. Did you hear that the Catholic Church took back Limbo. I guess it's a "never mind." I'm starting to wonder if there isn't a whole lot about the Catholic Church, about all organized religion that might turn out to be a "never mind."

And E. Howard Hunt says it was Lyndon Johnson and J. Edgar Hoover who organized the murder of John F. Kennedy.

This whole "land of the free" with killer jets flying over the stadium and everyone standing there with their hands over their hearts, tears in their eyes?

Never mind.

I stayed last night at the Jeannine Coallier Catholic Worker in Saginaw.

Thanks to Ellen Garrett for organizing my stay.

I met Tao this morning at the breakfast table. He took a break from watching his new robots movie to have some "crunch" toast. Another bright-eyed wonderful little kid.

Last night we had beers at Ewald's, a block from the 303. Marc showed me the table where he sits and writes poetry. He's good. Must be a great spot.

The back of Ellen's black Saturn is plastered with bumper stickers: War Is Not The Answer, Save The Farmland — No Wal-Mart, Thou Shall Not Kill, Bob Marley.

A few of them were recently keyed by someone, perhaps a disgruntled Wal-Mart greeter.

The Jeannine house has chickens in the yard.

Dawn of Dawn's coffee shop let us spend the afternoon drinking free coffee and peeing. She had to leave about five to go to a community event.

She said she opened the coffee shop a couple of years ago, in an area of Saginaw not popular for businesses, "because of crime."

She came down here because ...?

"To save the world."

She checked her bank account before going out, fifty dollars.

"Next week I'll make money. I think, someday it will come back to me. Which it will."

The sun is out.

George W. Bush is on the run, hiding from the truth, headed for a debacle that will put him in his historical prison cell for the rest of eternity.

You gotta love that.

It is indeed the dawn of a new day.

PTTPRO.

Note to self:
Yoda says, "The little bastards kill you must."

[chapter twenty-two]

Dostoyesky, Tolstoy, Dickens. I too
wanted to write in such a way that
people would see the injustices of
things as they were.

— Dorothy Day

CLEVELAND, OHIO — *KGB*.

It's a novel.

Saturday I spoke to a group at The Planet
bookstore in Ann Arbor. Glenn came up to me,
started touching all my books neatly arranged
on the table, and asked me, where's *KGB*?

I said I had written it a long time ago. It
was my first book.

The letters stand for Killing George Bush.

I've got one copy in the car, but that's it.

Oh.

I thought that was what this was all about,
he said.

Glenn said that Rush Limbaugh had said there
was this guy on a book tour around the country,
saying we should kill George Bush.

"I thought, this must be the guy!" he said.

Oh. Well. In the first place, I kind of
doubt that Limbaugh would even know who I am.

But, yeah, I guess that could be me.

I'm not looking to kill George Bush, but I did write a novel back around the turn of the century that does have that scenario as a premise.

KGB is set in the Woodbury County jail in Sioux City, Iowa. The prisoners are the main characters.

I wrote it about the time that Augusto Pinochet was being held somewhere for being a war criminal.

And I figured that we certainly have our own war criminals in the United States, and that if the truth were known about them, they would also be arrested and put on trial.

One of those is George Bush Sr.

In the novel, the inmates in the jail read about Pinochet in the one newspaper that is passed around to all the cell blocks, and they decide that Bush is also a war criminal.

They figure out that they have been hurt, attacked by Bush, and if not them personally, then at least persons on their side of the class struggle, warfare.

We really don't know what George Bush Sr. has done to us during his lifetime.

Some say he was involved in the murder of John F. Kennedy.

He says he was in Tyler, Texas that day, but others say he was registered at the Sheraton Hotel in Dallas. He says he was not a member of the CIA during that time.

Others point to evidence that says he was. There is also a photo that some say is Bush standing in front of the Texas School Book Depository after the assassination, on Nov. 22, 1963.

He says he was not involved in Iran-Contra.

Others say he was intensely involved.

He was a part of the movement of this country toward the boom in prison construction and incarceration, which put multitudes of non-violent offenders in prison for long, long prison terms, destroying families, under the guise of security, but really to further the political careers of people like George Bush Sr.

He ordered the invasion of Panama, which killed thousands, and what was the real reason for that? Will we ever know?

Do you remember the television shot of the Bush family before the Florida vote came in during the 2000 election? They were sitting around, smirking, scowling, knowing the fix was in, knowing, just knowing that they controlled this country, not the people.

And they were right.

And we can only speculate, imagine that George Bush Sr. was also involved in the planning and carrying out of 9-11.

Will we ever know?

Not unless the Democratic Party decides it wants to do its job.

We need a Truth Commission in this country. We need investigations, questions, questions, questions, prosecutions — perhaps prison sentences handed down.

And then maybe some of these so-called conspiracy theories will be rebuked.

But first, we need to find out who we really are.

We need to have real history taught in our schools.

Tell the truth to our children.

Tell them the truth about the Gulf of Tonkin, Pearl Harbor, 9-11, the Kennedy assassinations, the King murder, the death of Paul Wellstone, CIA drug running in the United States, etc. etc.

Did we really walk on the moon?

Yep, it sounds fantastic to doubt it.

But the reason it sounds unbelievable to some folks is because they do not think the

United States is capable of something like that.

Once you start to understand that we are capable of anything, then those sorts of questions don't seem quite so far-out.

At least — at least ask the questions, give the options, let the children know, let the adults know, that things might not be as we think they are.

If we could only air some of these things out, we might find out. We need to find out. We need to not be afraid of the answers.

Why? Why?

Why was the Bush administration so afraid of investigating 9-11?

Why did they have to be forced to investigate, and why was the investigation that did result so weak and orchestrated — designed to not get at the real truth. What are they afraid of?

Really.

Let us just have the truth.

We can't handle the lies any longer.

One of the first things George Bush Jr. did after 9-11 was to shut off access to presidential records of previous administra-

tions, including his father's. Why was that
necessary at that time?

It was not.

It was to cover-up, deceive.

And so I think it is plausible to explore in
a novel why and how an assassination might be
attempted, because the justice system is so
lacking — an attempt to bring about justice,
perhaps in the only way possible for certain
individuals.

It's a novel, asking questions, questions
that should have already been asked elsewhere,
making statements that should have already been
made elsewhere.

It's not about my wanting to kill George
Bush Sr., or wishing he would be killed.

It is wrong to kill.

I wish to God that George Bush Sr. knew
that.

My novel *KGB* is a creative endeavor that
tries to ask the question — why is the killing
of poor people taken so lightly and the idea
that they might some day seek revenge
considered so extraordinary?

[chapter twenty-three]

Indiana wants me. Lord, I can't go back there.

— Jesus

SUPER 8, INDIANA, USA — KGB.

A fantasy football team.

Killer Giant Ballerinas.

I am in Indiana, drove today from Cleveland to Bloomington's Boxcar Books, now headed toward Pittsburgh.

Yesterday I was a guest of the Cleveland Drinking Liberally group at Sullivan's Irish Pub on Madison Avenue.

I met Frederica and Dan, parents of Leonardo, eleven months old today [Monday].

Leonardo was born in Italy and has been in this country for two weeks. She is a doctor, he a "computer geek."

As we slowly make our way out of the bar, on the fancy wood flooring, past the cheering staff of Sullivan's Pub, Frederica and Dan point out to me things about Italy and the United States and democracy and stuff that make me think.

How do I find I-70? Is that east? That west?

Is this my nose? My ass?

Yeah-yeah, says Dan.

I love that yeah-yeah.

I started hearing it out this way. I'm going to keep listening for it.

The day before, I met with a Drinking Liberally group in a very northern suburb of Detroit, Ortonville.

I stayed with Ron and Nancy Wasczenski.

Well, I pulled up, into the long drive, the woods, the very nice house, with equestrian barn things around, affluence.

I did not feel like this was my place.

Remember, my comfort zone is sitting on the sofa with a yellow and red afghan pulled over my head.

Well, I got settled and the guests filtered in, sampling the horse doovers.

I was nervous, wondering how this would ever work.

But when it came time for me to speak I stood in front of the hundred-foot-wide TV in the downstairs recreation room with the bar and did my thing.

I talked about how Bush did 9-11 and the troops are just serving the empire and about sending a crossed-out tax form to the IRS before I left home.

Thank you for your time. Shuffle the papers.

Any questions? Comments?

Pause. Silence. Thousand one, thousand two.

"Have you seen the video *Loose Change*?" someone asked.

I breathed.

And we were off, talking about conspiracy this and controlled demolition that and had a great time.

Whew.

Marianna, who is a native of Montreal, and used to teach at the Flint performing arts high school, and now is a liturgical music planner for a local Lutheran church, said one of her students was a brother of Osama bin Laden.

Marianna would like to be a freeway blogger, she scoots over toward me on the sofa and confides, but she is afraid of being deported.

I had mentioned during my talk my previous difficulties in getting into Canada.

I wonder if I put up a sign against Bush I could get deported to Canada. No. That's not how it works. You are a dumbshit.

Yes. That's true. I'm sorry.

Doug, of Marianna and Doug, used to work for GM. He is now an antique dealer and does not miss GM.

He talks about how when you close a certain foreign car door, when it gets close to being closed, the car kind of takes it from there.

With a GM product, Doug says, it's "bam-bam-bam", okay, that fits now.

We all laugh. Doug makes us laugh a lot. He is a good guy. These are all good people now that I don't have to talk and can just sit and listen.

Doug knows Michael Moore, went to school with him, they were in chess club together.

Doug and Marianna have funny stories to tell about traveling in Europe, boating in Prague, shit like that.

Doug also works each week at a soup kitchen in downtown Detroit. He mentions the meth addicts that stop by.

"At least we're doing everything we can do."

Before they leave for the night Marianna takes my email address and says they might be able to give it to MM in L.A. sometime.

Awesome.

The Killer Giant Ballerinas are Ron's fantasy football league team. KGB took the league championship last year.

Ron — Waz — is a modern renaissance man.

He has a nice house, family, property. He is
an accountant. Hockey referee.

He is also an artist, a liberal, maybe
bordering on radical.

On his wall are original charcoal works of
art: Mark Fidrych, the Big Red Machine, Bob
Seger, Rod Stewart.

He is compassionate, passionate, connected.

Someone who could run for office, network
with the local Democratic Party big whigs, and
also hoot and holler and get home late from a
Black Oak Arkansas concert.

He is a Michigan boy, played hockey,
football, eats McDonald's by the bucket full,
can drink beer with either hand. Knows all the
eff about Chomsky and Zinn and whatever else
liberal crap you got.

He lets me into his home to talk about my
books, talk bad about George Bush, drink his
beer, eat his shrimp. He cares. He's trying.
He's doing good things. He's going to do lots
more good things.

He says that he met Joe Wilson of Valerie
Plame Wilson at some function.

Joe said: "There are no tinfoil hats. These
guys can do anything."

Do-do. Do-do. Do-do. Do-do.

I am impressed, but I'm glad to be gone.

I'm always glad to be gone.

Remember my comfort zone? I always feel lucky to talk to the people I meet.

I don't know what they think about me, but I am happy to be able to say what's on my mind.

And I'm also always very happy to get back into the rusty, brown Honda and put on the headphones and dial up the Dixie Chicks or Steve Earle to celebrate the freedom of the road, being alone, on the way, going somewhere, else.

Well, I took I-75 Sunday through the heart of Detroit, past Comerica Stadium.

I was able to get the Twins-Tigers for a short time on my headphones.

I can't help but stare right and left at the city, at the neighborhoods.

Poverty is interesting. Affluence is boring.

I wonder about what goes on in that house, down that street, in that park.

I drove around Kansas City in the black neighborhood I was going to read in, Milwaukee, Minneapolis. I just don't understand why we allow poverty. I just don't get it.

Some people live in these types of neighborhoods and we all just accept it.

I remember doing a story on Mexicans in Minnesota who lived in a goddamn compound, like a prison camp, for a portion of the year, just to work for one of the canning companies.

Geezuz-eff! What is wrong with us?

Look out for the big-effing truck.

And I want to write something that saves all the poor people.

Sure.

I know they don't need me.

I still want to write that novel.

A good book could bring George W. Bush to his knees.

A novel has the potential power to save the world.

It does.

Maybe not my novel.

But maybe yours.

Think about it.

Today I drove from Cleveland to Bloomington and got skunked at Boxcar Books.

I was headed to Pittsburgh this evening, stopped on the Interstate somewhere. I can only hope I'm out of Indiana.

Geezuz.

It was one million degrees in Bloomington this afternoon.

The drive from Martinsville down to Bloomington on 37 South is really pretty cool.

The trees are beginning to bud. I used to rely on Rosey to tell me things like that. Now I have to notice that shit for myself.

I spotted a Big Red Liquor store. Reminded me of Nebraska.

Oh, God.

I think all the fervor spikes the temperature a bit.

There was this billboard promoting the upcoming National Day of Prayer, May something-or-other.

"Americans Unite In Prayer."

Nah. Eff that.

Unite toward what? More war? A longer wall along the Mexican border? Big Red Boo-ya?

Instead.

Put George W. Bush in D Unit behind the walls in Terre Haute Penitentiary for lying to us about WMDs and getting 3,500 Americans killed, for murdering Paul Wellstone, and for attacking his own country on 9-11-01.

And give him a fourth count for just being a dumb-eff.

Praise the Lord. Pass the red T-shirts.

I went walking around Bloomington before my sucky gig at Boxcar Books.

It was another funky area, like in Madison, Ann Arbor, Lawrence.

In all these towns I like to take a little walk if I can, because I will never-ever see any of these places again. Rosey has assured me.

And so I wore my "Worst President Ever" T-shirt over to the University of Indiana campus and walked around.

Revolutionary.

Nah, just some old guy with no job walking around where he doesn't belong in a black T-shirt on a scorching hot day.

But, back here in the hotel zone on the interstate, wherever I am, the woman who took my money for gas said her boyfriend would like my T-shirt and where did I get it. Then the woman who checked me into the motel said, "I like your T-shirt."

God Bless Indiana.

I wonder.

[chapter twenty-four]

I opened up my eyes, took a look around.
I saw it written across the sky. The
Revolution Starts Now.

— Steve Earle

SWALESVILLE, PA — "I don't like today's
world. There's going to be two kinds of people
rich people and poor people."

I was sitting in the Joseph-Beth bookstore
in Pittsburgh on Tuesday, scanning through John
Updike's book "The Terrorist," cozied up in a
soft chair, kind of listening to these three
older people.

Older than me?

I'd like to think so.

I then went and put some more quarters into
the meter so the Pittsburgh police don't hide
my car.

Then I walk over and sit next to the
fountain out in the little plaza outside The
Cheesecake Factory in this square on Cinema
Drive. I watch some kids get wet and then walk
over to Claddagh Irish pub.

It's not like the Irish pub in Kansas City,
more like the one in Cleveland, trendy, lots of
shiny wood, brass. I'd rather be in the K.C.

bar, which was a dive, maybe the ultimate dive bar.

You could picture Irish revolutionaries, fighters, drinking in that bar. Not here.

That's just me.

At Claddagh's I meet with Dave and John and Halley.

Dave is from Boston. He says caah and baah.

I have never heard anyone say caah and baah in person. I have never been anywhere. I think it is pretty cool. I try to get him to say more things.

What's in the sky at night?

Peanut butter comes in a ...?

He tires of my game.

Halley drove One Hundred Miles to see me.

I shake her hand, maybe three or four times before the night is over. She is a carpenter. She has Band Aids on at least four of her fingers, robins-egg blue maybe.

Dave and John talk about politics, presidential candidates.

Dave went to CMU, Carnegie Melon University, studied engineering.

He admits to being a geek. I agree.

We — they — talk about the various
Democratic candidates. I don't have much to
offer. The subject doesn't excite me.

I would be for any candidate who would get
us out of Iraq yesterday, initiate a brand new
investigation of 9-11, and investigate the
present administration as regards to possible
war crimes: lying to start a war, torture,
secret prisons.

Investigate the death of Paul Wellstone.

Point me toward the candidate who will do
that.

Otherwise, the whole thing is pretty boring,
more interesting to watch the Cubs and Pirates
on the TV above the expensive bar counter. 5-2,
Cubs.

Hey.

On the way to Pittsburgh from Indianapolis,
I came through Wheeling, West Virginia.

Tell me if you know — wasn't Wheeling the
hometown of Chris Stevens of Chris in the
Morning on KBHR radio of Cicily, Alaska on
"Northern Exposure."

Well, there was a detour on I-70 that took
us right through downtown.

Wheeling is a Wow-Town, at least for me —
the old buildings, the trees, the hills, the
history that I can only imagine quickly in my
mind as I try to keep up with the maroon car
that I think knows where we are going.

It reminds me of Lead and Deadwood, South
Dakota, built into the hills.

Well, I did make it to Pittsburgh and that
is another Wow-Town.

Maybe it's because I just haven't been
anywhere, but I think you would also agree,
that coming out of the Fort Pitt Tunnel and
then boom! there is a big bridge, a big river
and boom! the skyline of Pittsburgh, all right
there.

Like plowing into an I-Max Theatre.

You want to come back and do it again and
again, just to see that view, but you can't,
there are one million maroon cars behind you
that don't care about your Iowa license to
drive slow. You have to keep going.

Or die.

And so I keep going and, of course, I miss
my MapQuest directions by one turn, but that is
enough to put me smack-dab into rush hour traffic, then try to find a place to turn around in
Monroeville [the shocks?], then I go past the
immigrants' rights rally, and then I pass it
again and again ... and again, and I am starting to get to know these people ... and final-

ly pull over and ask this British guy and this Hispanic-looking woman for help who are very intent on finding a parking place and get to the rally, but they do find time to tell me where to go.

I find Hot Metal Street.

Turn right, miss my next turn, and I go up and up and up.

Pittsburgh is hilly. Did you know that? And the streets where I am are very tight.

I am panicking, as I do when I think I am lost in rush hour in a big city that I have never been in and I might die soon because I cannot find a fancy Irish bar.

My brakes feel squishy. Does that mean my brakes are going out? My clutch? Pittsburgh is the end of the line. I am dead. Oh, geezuz-god, my brakes are squishy. I will die.

I am again in the black neighborhood. In almost every city I visit I either miss my turn and go to the black neighborhood, or my reading is in the black neighborhood.

I like it here. I calm down. I wish I had some excuse to walk up to someone and listen to them talk about their day.

I ask directions once, from a guy walking down a hill.

... I almost make it.

I seek directions again, from a woman in front of what I would guess is a project. She is very kind, she turns and points, tells me to go to Josephine Street, then to 26th, down the hill, "you can't miss ... "

No, no, don't say that!

"it."

I later try to ask directions from a white young man walking intently down the narrow sidewalk.

"Fuck you."

From the truck turning the corner: "Wake up, buddy!"

Dude. I'm doing the best I — fuck you, too!

I find the rich Irish bar and a parking spot and put in dozens of quarters even though the police don't check meters this late in the day. If I don't put dozens of quarters in, I will die.

And so now I can relax. I know where I need to be. I have time. I go to the bookstore to look around, relax, find a restroom. Rest.

There are escalators in Joseph-Beth, just like in the Rochester, Minnesota Barnes & Noble, very cool.

I look around. I can't really afford any of the books, but I look.

And it seems like they don't mind, so I grab "The Terrorist," and go find a nice place to rest for just awhile. There is a restroom up the escalator. I'm good.

I know it's just me, and I'm not well-read enough, but I don't see what is so special about Updike's book.

And I read one called "Absurdistan" somewhere else and on the back cover they have blurbs from the Washington Post Book World and ten other newspapers that I could not get to look at my books if I included a staah in a jaah.

"The Terrorist" is okay, but it's not one of my books.

Sorry. I really believe that.

My books should be in these places.

They are just as good, better.

Why they aren't here, I can only say has to do with the structure of the book industry, which I probably don't fully understand.

I'm as good as Updike, as anyone, but no agent or major publishing company would give me directions out of town.

Of course I would say that, right? What it really has to do with is story and characters and pacing and lots of stuff, right?

Okay, if it does, fine. But I really don't get it.

Maybe smart guys get it. I do not.

So I don't die.

I park. I live. I put hundreds of quarters into the meter.

And I go talk to the Democrats.

They are gracious. They have allowed me to meet with them.

Of course I am grateful.

But I don't see any hope in the Democratic Party.

I ran for Congress in Iowa in 2000 as a Democrat. I won the primary and received 67,000 votes in the general election on an anti-military, anti-prison, pro-Hispanic immigration, in a very conservative district.

But that's not what Democrats generally do.

Usually they stick their finger into the air, judge the wind, and run thataway.

Rather than looking into their hearts and then walking confidently out the front door, no matter which way the wind is blowing.

And then they die.

[chapter twenty-five]

There are things we don't or can't understand. A reasonable man, a healthy man ... a sane man ... when he encounters the inexplicable ... forgets about it.

> — Maurice Minnifield, *Northern Exposure*

BUFFALO UNIVERSITY, BUFFALO, NEW YORK — Nancy Pelosi is hot.

I have noticed I am surging toward old-guy status. Women who used to be the principal or someone's nice grandmother on the porch in the blue flower dress down to her ankles now kind of get me going.

Oh, God.

Nancy is on C-Span right now, talking about stuff.

So was the woman running for president in France just a minute ago. Lots of stuff.

You should have seen this debate between the two candidates for president of France or whatever they call it, premier, general secretary, bunga-bunga-something-something.

They were really going at it, discussing, arguing. It was not controlled. There were no microphones in their ears or packs on their

backs where smarter people told them what to
say.

They say America is a model for democracy
for the world.

Not.

I used to think Hillary was hot.

I don't anymore. I don't know why. Things
just kind of cooled.

Nancy has just said we need to rebuild our
military.

She still looks pretty good to me.

Hey.

Dude.

I am staying in this effing guest house on
the campus of the University of Buffalo, The
Center For Inquiry, in Buffa-effing-lo. Not bad
for a guy who graduated 283 out of 289 from New
Field High School in 1973.

Well, it's not a chauffeur and caviar on
Ritz crackers, but definitely I'll take it. I
drove this morning [Wednesday] from Pittsburgh.
I am from New Field and I have not travelled
all that much, so please excuse me.

THERE WERE TREES AND HILLS AND A BIG-EFFING
LAKE AND IT WAS WAAAY COOL.

I don't know, it's just exciting to see some things.

I was traveling today on the Blue Star Memorial Highway. "Dedicated to those who fought for ... blah, blah, blah ..." Oh, God, did I fall asleep for a moment there? How many of these effing things do we have around?

A whole effing-bunch.

Methinks we protest too much.

> Anyone STUPID enough to join the military ...
>
> ought to be able to.
>
> — Bill Hicks

I think we know the military is a bunch of hired thugs, paid killers, that do not protect us, but rob and rape and kill in order to secure markets for American business, and we build all these memorials — like someone who has just committed some crime just keeps on talking and talking, because he knows as soon as he shuts up, he is going to be found out.

I don't know. Or else they are effing heroes for killing millions of people and making sure that we are able to gamble in the casino of our choice.

Well, for those who didn't know — everybody
but me — western Pennsylvania is hilly and
there are vineyards and shit. And Niagara Falls
billboards. I am on Interstate 90, which goes
all the way back to Sioux Falls, which is near
my home. When I was in prison in Texas in 1986
I used to look out over the prison yard at
night and see the full moon and reassure myself
by thinking that Rosey was seeing the same
moon, even though it seemed we were not even
inhabiting the same world, we were so far
apart.

Well, Interstate 90 runs all the way back
home and so maybe I'm not so far away.

"Correctional Facility. Don't Pick Up Hitch-
hikers."

I pass that sign somewhere headed toward
Buffalo and I cross myself.

I used to cross myself when I passed a
Catholic Church. My mother did that and so I
did it.

But it was pretty stupid.

However, crossing yourself when you pass a
prison makes a little more sense.

There is so much evil and suffering inside a
prison that it makes more sense than doing it
when you pass in front of Sacred Heart Church.
The prison is more holy. Not because of it
being a prison. But because of the suffering.

I find my way into Buffalo, Main Street, Talking Leaves Books. I shake hands with Jonathon, the owner, with whom I have exchanged emails for the past one hundred years trying to set this up.

I read and then go over to Buffalo University.

David Mussella directs me to The Center For Inquiry.

He parks at the edge of the lot.

Why?

If they bomb us, at least I'll be able to get to my car.

Bomb? Who? Why? While I'm here? Big bombs? Maybe little, teeny-weeny bombs?

David says the center is about secular humanism, which pisses some people off.

I don't really know what secular humanism is, but I don't mention it, because I have heard they have this private guest house I get to stay in.

And there's more to it than that, but I kind of lose interest.

David shows me inside and introduces me to Joe Nickell.

Joe takes me to his office as I listen for bombs.

He immediately begins to tell me that he is
a paranormal investigator.

"I'm not a believer," he says.

In what?

His small office is packed with green blow-up
alien dolls, voodoo figure things with things
sticking into them, bigfoot foot plaster casts,
leprechaun posters.

There are caps from "Unsolved Mysteries."

"We have a laboratory."

There it is.

Joe tells me right off that he does not
believe in ghosts because, "where does the
brain go."

I'm like, I dunno.

He says that Hilary Swank is starring in a
new movie based on his work.

"It's a terrible movie, though," he says.

I tell Joe that I've probably seen him on
TV.

He says that could very well be true — and
he has written twenty-one books.

There they are.

On the desk is a magazine: Fatima Mysteries.

What about Roswell? I ask.

Military balloons.

No alien bodies. Hoax.

He also implies that those who believe the Bush people were involved in 9-11 are also quite delusional.

I shift my feet, stand up straight.

That makes me feel a bit unsettled. I don't want to be wrong, a fool.

I believe in Bigfoot, UFOs. I believe Bush did it.

But ... you know ... it's not about that, is it?

What it is, it is.

I really believe that.

The truth is what is important.

It is not important that certain beliefs be sustained, regardless.

The truth.

In debates, UFOs, Bigfoot, starting wars.

I am in favor. I vote yes.

Show me where it shows that Dick Cheney did not kill all those people in the Twin Towers and I'm heading home this morning, back to

Iowa, to sit on the patio and pet my cat and sip beer from a quart bottle staring at my lovely wife mowing the lawn.

That night [Wednesday] I was part of the Literary Cafe at the University of Buffalo. It's a regular thing where people get together to read their poems and stuff.

Mostly it's writers reading to each other is what I figure.

It is damn hard to get anyone else to listen.

But still, it's good. For one thing, it's good to know these people are out there, writing their poems. They are like the monks in a mona- stery, praying, and having that praying somehow help us all.

I really enjoy the chance to read. There are about twenty people there. I have developed the habit of counting people so that I can report to Rosey how many were there. I'll find myself in a men's restroom on the Interstate thinking, one, two, three-four, five-six-seven — this would make a pretty good crowd.

The podium has a lamp on it. There is [are?] cheese and crackers in the hall. Before I read I was nervous because there were so many people and Joe Nickell, the debunker guy — who is also a good poet — was in the audience and practi- cally everything I talk about is about ghosts and spirits and little green leprechauns flying big white planes into buildings.

But just before I walk up there I realize, I like this shit. I like doing this. I still get nervous. I am still maybe not real great at it, but I think I have good material and maybe I'm learning how to deliver it.

I think we have a history of being lied to by our government. I think we have too many war memorial highways for no good-goddamn reason.

And I can't make myself forget about it.

[chapter twenty-six]

I don't care if it rains or freezes,
long as I got my plastic Jesus, ridin'
on the dashboard of my car.

    — Cool Hand Luke

NEW YORK CITY — If I can make it here, I'll make it anywhere.

I got skunked Friday night at Bluestockings Books in New York City.

Oh, well.

Right now I'm sitting in Everything Goes Books & Cafe in Staten Island. It's Saturday afternoon. A beautiful day.

Did I tell you?

I was in Rochester, New York on Thursday, then drove down to NYC for my evening debacle on the Lower East Side.

I don't think I told you.

I crossed myself about a hundred times and then drove into New York City in the brown Honda yesterday afternoon. That car, if it were a person, deserves most of the credit for me getting this far on this trip.

What heart that old soul has, seven thousand miles already, 170,000-plus all-told.

Actually drove into the city, through the city, down the Palisades Parkway, the FDR,

across the Williamsburg Bridge, into Brooklyn.
I was going under the train, on the street. It
reminded me of some movies, maybe "Finding
Nemo," maybe "The French Connection."

And I think about Jimmy Breslin, going all-
effing around these freaking neighborhoods,
with his tie loose, his shirttail out, his hair
stickin' out every-friggin'-way, a pad in one
hand, pen in the other, walking fast, headed to
his desk to punch out literature with two
fingers, on deadline.

I got lost and stopped to ask for
directions, twice.

The people were extra nice. I kind of knew
they would be. Rosey and the kids and I had
been to New York over New Year's. We saw
"Hairspray" and walked around Times Square for
four days. The people in the city were nice.

The cab driver talked to us about Queens and
Harlem and the bridges we passed as we stared
out the windows trying to take it all in.

And the New York drivers were not the eleven
-headed monsters the folks in Rochester had
told me about.

I made it to Jim Fleming's place in
Brooklyn.

Jim lives there with his partner Lewanne
Jones in an old warehouse building. It's huge.

It used to be a publishing house, back in
the 1800s. I think he said McLaughlin House.

They published children's books, then moved to
board games when that became more profitable.
One of their games was a puzzle called "*Chopped
Up Niggers*." Then they either moved somewhere
else or they got real jobs, I dunno.

Anyway, Jim and Lewanne moved in about
twenty-five years ago and live in this huge
loft with walls made out of books and a view of
Manhattan, the Brooklyn Bridge, the Hudson
River.

For about the first hour when you walk into
this place you just say "Wow" about one million
times.

Jim is a small press publisher, Autonomedia.

He is originally from Clear Lake, Iowa, not
so far east of where I live now in Iowa.

Lewanne does research work for documentary
films. She worked on the PBS *Eyes on the Prize*
series, and also *Fahrenheit 911*. Her name is on
the credits. She is working now on something
about the life of George H.W. Bush.

On 9-11-01 Jim watched the burning buildings
out his living room window. Their son was in a
school about a block from the burning
buildings.

You know the first time you drive into
anywhere it's like, I LOVE this effing place.
And then after you meet some people, do some
things, maybe you change your mind. Maybe you
don't and you stay twenty-five years.

Well, me driving into Brooklyn on this sunny day in May, it's like, "It's A Beautiful Day In The Neighborhood!" There are Hasidic Jewish people all over, and I can see that some of them live in these huge high-rise buildings, and there is the neighborhood grocery store, and there is a Mom with her kids and the grandpa.

And I'm pumping my brake, down-shifting, looking here and there, searching for Big Bird and Elmo.

That's just me. I like Sesame Street. I like the Barney show. You know why? Because I remember watching those shows with the kids when they were young. They've outgrown them. Doesn't appear that I have.

That was pretty cool. I was so worried about driving into New York City and then it was fine.

Jim accompanied me to my reading over on Allen Street. He and Lewanne moved into their neighborhood when it was much more dangerous than it is now. Now it is dangerous because they are being forced out by a raise in rents.

On one of the pillars in the kitchen there are height marks for their kids Ryder and Bronwyn, up, up, up. Now those kids are in college.

Jim moved here from Iowa to be with this wonderful woman and it worked.

Well, down at Bluestockings they set up all
these effing chairs and I want to say, no,
maybe don't do that.

I talk to Jacob because he has read my T-
shirt: *No Seriously, Why Did We Invade Iraq?*

He is a young man with a blond mohawk. He
shows me the anarchist "A" he has etched
permanently into his left forearm. I ask him if
he is glad he did it. He says, yes. His eyes
say, I dunno.

That time leading up to a reading is always
tense, especially when it really looks like
nobody is going to show up. There's nothing you
can do about it, though. I'm a writer, not a
magician or a harmonica player or a rodeo
clown. It's a novel, not a new brand of beer,
or movie, or car.

Anyway, I decide it's time to fold it up. We
go over to another part of town, the Brecht
Forum, where one million people are sitting and
listening to Grace Lee Boggs.

It was a boring talk.

Sorry.

I had never heard of her. Probably my own
fault.

These people should have been over at
Bluestockings listening to me.

She was talking about Malcolm and Martin
Luther King Jr. and a million years ago, how to

build nurturing relationships, and ... zzz ...
zzz. It's naptime in the neighborhood.

There was nobody to hear me talk about
stopping the war, impeaching George Bush,
putting George Bush in Terre Haute Penitentiary
and finding out how Dick Cheney planned and
carried out 9-11.

I'm supposed to be a gracious loser, say
that I understand this. I am nobody, and Grace
Lee Boggs is an icon and zzz ... zzz.

They had wine and cheese and crackers, and
thanks for that, but, well, I don't remember
much else. I must have blacked out.

In Rochester on Thursday, after drinking
with the Democrats at Monty's Korner I got
pulled over by a giant Rochester police man.

I was not drunk, had two beers during five
of the longest hours of my life, so the reason
I failed to stay in my own lane was because I
was so tired and bored with Democrats, not the
two glasses of Guinness.

Sir. [He shines his giant cop flashlight
into my eyes, which is supposed to help you to
think, I guess.] *Have you been talking to
Democrats?*

Yeah, I mumble.

How many?

I dunno. Four, five, six.

Would you step out of the car, sir?

Please place your index finger, sir, next to your lips, run it up and down and go "bbb-bbb-bbb."

Scared the shit out of me. Couldn't find my registration, anything. *Why are you here?* Book tour. *What kind of a book tour?* There are kinds? *How long have you owned this car?* I would have to ask Rosey. *Where are you going?*

Some Democrat's house.

Oh, well, now I am on/in Staten Island. My reading is in one hour and then I am going to find my shorts and some beer and go sit by the water like an old man should.

I am staying at something called the Ganas Community, on Scribner Street in/on Staten Island. The owners of the bookstore are members here. I guess Ganas is Spanish for having the will to do something, in other words, the balls, the cajones.

I'm here for one night for twenty-five dollars and laundry is free and food, too. They have businesses owned-in-common on the island and they have a bunch of houses and kids running around and everyone greets you and smiles and a garden and shit. And already I need to get away from here.

I guess they started about twenty-five years ago when some people from San Francisco wanted to live together, moved to New York City, then over to Staten Island where the housing was easier to come by.

Aviva just showed me around. She is having her fifty-first birthday tomorrow and the community is having a picnic down by the water. She is from Argentina and Israel, has been here three years.

Later I meet someone working on the house who has been here since 1991. Geezuz-god.

Then I talk to Robert, who has just moved into the community. He drives a rickshaw in Manhattan, charges people twenty-five dollars a ride. Some are tourists, some really need to get places.

I'm not going to ask if I can bring in the rest of my twenty-four pack of Coors that's heating in the backseat of my car. Better to apologize than ask permission. Didn't Geronimo say that?

Oh, well.

Did you know that Staten Island is pretty large and at least the part that I am on is extremely hilly? The Honda is parked on Scribner Street and looks like an old car on the launch pad ready for lift-off. It wants to go, is ready for the journey, willing.

May we all have the ganas to do what we really want to do.

It is a beautiful day on the island.

Aloha.

[chapter twenty-seven]

We Earth Men have a talent for ruining
big, beautiful things. The only reason
we didn't set up hot-dog stands in the
midst of the Egyptian temple of Karnak
is because it was out of the way and
served no large commercial purpose.

  - *The Martian Chronicles*, Ray
    Bradbury

STATEN ISLAND, NY — "He's been compared to
Kurt Vonnegut in his writing."

That's Steve of ETG Books & Cafe in/on
Staten Island trying to entice a woman and her
daughter to sit the eff down and listen to me
talk.

I am up on the stage, planting my butt on
the bar stool, figuring out how to put my
papers on the podium, messing with the
microphone, wondering which way is home.

The woman smiles and heads back out the door
to the sidewalk.

There is just no denying it, this book tour
is a loser.

There have been some great moments, and I
always-always meet great people everywhere, by
one's and by two's.

But there are many times when nobody shows
up. On a great day, on a bad day, would you go

out of your way to listen to somebody talk
about a book? It would have to be Kurt
Vonnegut, right?

And, well, now you might as well stay home.

Well, I sit up on the stage and give my
talk. I speak loud into the microphone, hoping
my words — Impeach George Bush, Investigate the
Bush administration's involvement in 9-11 — get
out onto the street where there are lots of
people.

Afterward, I sit down on the edge of the
stage and mingle with the crowd: co-manager
Steve, Dennis, while other co-manager Katie
goes to do some work.

We talk. Dennis asks about my sanctuary
thing with the bishop and the cathedral and the
federal government in Omaha in the 1980s.

Dennis is tallish, thin, wearing a black
ballcap with a red "L", dark sunglasses to the
middle of his nose. He used to be a teacher in
New York City. He's wearing a big class ring
from somewhere. His jeans are worn. He wears
tennis shoes with no socks.

Steve wonders whether it would be more
productive to be "for peace" rather than
"against war."

Somehow we start talking about 9-11.

Dennis says he was watching it all from
Skyline Park in Staten Island. His wife was on

a plane from Newark, and at the time he was not sure if hers was one of the planes that had hit the towers.

Dennis and Steve doubt the government's story about 9-11. Dennis talks about how the buildings came down, that if the heat truly melted the steel it would have come down twisting and irregular, like hot taffy, not straight down.

They say that New Yorkers are divided in their views on what the truth is about 9-11.

Then they talk about the honey bees. Where did the honey bees go and did I hear about that?

No.

Maybe something about Monsanto products and killing the bees and now lots of stuff doesn't get pollinated and grow, and where did the honey bees go?

I really don't know.

Dennis says it has to do with lack of truth and love in human thought.

I go for a walk after my talk, carrying a plain bagel with humus [wtf?] and cream cheese, made by Steve, over toward the Staten Island Ferry.

I find a mailbox to send a letter to Rosey. I kiss the envelope before dropping it in,

seems appropriate, but I still look around to
see if anyone saw me.

Somebody at a light leans over to the open
passenger window.

"Where'd you get that shirt?"

It says, "No, Seriously, Why Did We Invade
Iraq?"

I say, "Online."

The black man smiles, nods, gives me the
thumbs-up.

"Nice shirt."

I smile wide inside.

This T-shirt is a winner.

Then I go find a bench to eat my bagel,
drink the rest of my warm Diet Mountain Dew and
listen to a black family next to me argue, then
laugh, banter, play. I look out at the water
and Manhattan, and barges.

Then I go buy some rice at "Spanish Restaurant."

Loser. Quixotic. Long Shot.

You know, when I ran for Congress in 2000 as
a Democrat I asked a good friend to help me
with the campaign. I thought it would be fun,
and was a hell of a good opportunity to say
something strong to the Democrats and Repub-

licans. The friend said, no, it sounded like a
quixotic venture.

What?

I thought that was kind of the point.

Going to prison to stop the United States
military is kind of quixotic, too. But we still
did it, because it's good and right and just
and strong.

And it's worthwhile. Even if your whole life
is "just a good try," that is still pretty
good.

I think.

I'd like to be a winner. Who wouldn't?

You would not choose to be a loser, but
really, that's where the interesting people
are.

But you kind of have to be forced to meet
them, to have those experiences. It's like when
you take a wrong turn, or run out of gas, or
have a flat tire, and later, it's not so bad,
you met so and so, did this and that. If it
were up to you, to me, the only folks you would
meet would be on the first tee, the first row
at the ballpark, the front row of the theater.

When it's the people selling the popcorn you
really need to get to know.

A loser doesn't mean not worthwhile. Losers are not worthless, they just don't win very often.

They still play, right? They still come to the ballpark.

They sit on the park bench, likely alone, wondering where the honey bees have gone. And sometimes, sometimes, they turn out to be the rejected stone that becomes the cornerstone.

So, tomorrow I go to Rhode Island.

[chapter twenty-eight]

I ain't got no home. I'm just a ramblin'
round,

I go from town to town.

— Woody Guthrie

NOT IN PROVIDENCE, RHODE ISLAND — These
perfect towns of Connecticut make me want to
puke.

Yesterday I was heading toward Providence on
I-95. I started to shake, sweat, and pulled the
Honda off onto the exit for Madison, Conn.
After waiting for one hundred traffic lights I
saw to my right a big yard, maybe a park. I
pulled around, down the lane, hurried out and
got on one knee and dry-heaved on the front
lawn of the First Congregational Church of
Madison.

You would think the yard would be filled
with folks leaning out their windows, beside
their cars, on both knees, hurling — to see
this sight. This humongous white church: six
pillars on the front porch that two strong men
could not reach around and touch pinky fingers.

And behind the pillars, blowing in the
breeze. Of course, a gigantic American flag.

This is turning into the "Why I Hate America
Tour."

I thought I hated America because of its being a killer. Turns out there are more specific reasons.

Indiana. Democrats. Connecticut.

And I can't get into Canada because I am not rehabilitated from my jail terms in the 1980s. I sent in a crossed-out tax form before I left to protest against Bush & Cheney & Rove killing all those Americans on 9-11.

I will soon be wanted in New York State for not paying a stay in your own lane buddy ticket. I did not pay my parking ticket in Iowa City a few weeks ago.

And now I am wanted in Rhode Island for failure to appear.

Well, I didn't make it to Providence because I was too sick to drive. Too many cans of Coors in the New Haven Days Inn. No joke. Poisoning myself. How stupid is that?

And therefore, I think that this is an excellent time for us to talk about the rotten churches we have in this country.

From *Wake the Eff Up From The American Dream*:

A woman pastor from Franklin:

We Christians will bomb and rape and steal and lie. We might as well call ourselves tree trimmers as Christians. We have turned it into a nonsense word.

We will sit there and listen to the pastor. He dares say nothing about the poor or poverty or our own riches and home, our ultimate concern for our own undisturbed routines — nothing about building bombs to kill rather than bread to feed, and Oh, God, we do not remind him.

He will never mention Thou Shall Not Kill or the true spirit of Christianity and this will be repeated week after week in thousands of churches around the country and we shall never be bothered with the real you, Jesus, who would rather see these crystal crappers laid down brick upon brick and our own phony hearts torn from our chests, because we are scoundrels, Lord.

This morning I am at the Econo Lodge in Groton, Connecticut, the home of a humongous United States submarine base. Last night as I was searching for the ball game on the television I came across The Pentagon Channel.

The woman announcer had on a military uniform.

At least she was honest. I would think Dan Rather, Tom Brokaw and Peter Jennings could have been as truthful in their on-camera attire.

Well, last night I had the Yankees-Mariners game on TV with no sound as I watched a docu-mentary on my laptop about the John Kennedy murder.

Put out by the History Channel, it is
probably twenty-five years old by now, but a
lot of it is the same as what has recently
appeared regarding Lyndon Baines Johnson's
involvement in killing his boss.

The actor Bruce Willis has recently said
that he believes some of those involved in the
Kennedy murder are still in the United States
government.

I agree.

I remember when I was a kid in New Field,
Nebraska in the 1960s when all this was
happening. Back then we were certain Oswald did
it.

The New Field Daily News told us so, the
network news told us so, hometown hero Johnny
Carson told us so, and Sacred Heart Catholic
Church told us so.

Dan Rather saw the Zapruder film and assured
us the shots came from behind. And then they
hid the film for a hundred years.

It would have been considered insane to even
consider that any of the shots came from the
grassy knoll area.

Now we learn it was Lyndon-effing-Johnson
who did it? And that he met the night before,
in Texas, with a bunch of oil tycoons, J. Edgar
Hoover, Richard Nixon and who knows who else?
Whom?

And when he came out of the meeting he told his mistress, "those s.o.b.'s will never embarrass me again."

Maybe from Vermont I will tell you about the letter I received from Johnny Carson when I asked him about his television interview with Jim Garrison.

Can you imagine what secrets about the current government wait to be revealed? Some that perhaps connect the killings of the 1960s with today's headlines?

And that is why I need to go to Brattleboro today and keep plugging away on this tour.

Remember what Joe Wilson told Ron from Detroit?

"There are no tinfoil hats. These people are capable of anything."

When we really discover the truth about the death of Paul Wellstone, 9-11, the anthrax, the murders of the Kennedy brothers, Martin Luther King Jr., the presidential elections of 2000, 2004 — the front lawns of all the churches in America will be running with puke.

[chapter twenty-nine]

There was always a minority afraid of
something, and a great majority afraid
of the dark, afraid of the future,
afraid of the past, afraid of the
present, afraid of themselves and
shadows of themselves.

> — *The Martian Chronicles*, Ray
> Bradbury

Picture Window View, IOWA — You want to go
where everybody knows your name.

Well.

I was in Boston last week. I made my way
through traffic, found a parking spot, found
the Lucy Parsons Center, on Columbus Avenue.
Then I went out walking around for about seven
hours. Part of the time I just sat on a bench
at a park, watched the people and the pigeons.

And then I walked over to Lucy Parsons, came
up to the front desk, tired, sweating, lugging
my books and stuff.

"I'm Allen.

"Allen. T. Alyan.

"I'm supposed to speak tonight."

"Oh, was that tonight?"

It's kind of been like that on this book tour.

In Brattleboro, Vermont there were naked people outside the bookstore. But nobody inside at my reading.

This isn't Home, Iowa. I work in Home, at a group home. It's very conservative. It's what drove me to write *Wake the Eff Up From* The American Dream how these people live during this time of war.

I don't think the naked people were Dutch Reformed. Maybe they just weren't big readers. And so now I'm back home in Iowa taking a short break before the rest of the tour, writing this last column from my daughter's computer.

Mine crashed somewhere in Connecticut.

I need to get it fixed before sailing on.

I started to plan this tour back in October.

Then I left home in March. Now I'm back home in May.

It's been like that.

I thought that if I got out there and bit the bullet, spoke in front of crowds, I could get people to notice the books I have written.

There must be another way. Maybe I just haven't found it. Maybe it's right there in front of me, but not clearly marked, or marked at all, or hidden behind a FREAKING LILAC BUSH,

like the sign for the road out of Brockton,
Massachusetts.

I did meet great people.

But this first part of the trip was a loser.
There's no denying that. A good attitude only
gets you as far as Boston.

I'm not really sure what the answer is. It
could be that people don't read novels.

But who really knows about that. It could be
that they just don't read mine, or that
readings are just too boring. I have never been
to a reading, other than my own. It does sound
like maybe the most boring thing you can think
of, if someone asked you to think of five
boring things, or ten, and it was against the
rules to make the Democratic Party all ten.

The brown 1990 Honda was great. Nine
thousand, eight hundred seventy-six miles. No
problem. I saw other brown Hondas on the road
and all had the same rust in the rear wheel
wells.

Do-do, do-do, do-do.

Whatever.

I think the answer is don't quit.

Really.

Get naked, join the Dutch Reformed Church,
and read.

[chapter thirty]

If we long to believe that the stars
rise and set for us, that we are the
reason there is a Universe, does science
do us a disservice in deflating our
conceits?

    — Carl Sagan

TULSA, OK — "Fuck the FCC. Fuck the FBI.
Fuck the CIA. I'm livin' in the mother-fuckin'
USA."

Wouldn't you feel more like standing if that
Steve Earl song were the National Anthem?

And it's not anti-patriotic. It's very
patriotic, more in line with the Founding
Fathers than what we have going on today.

What we have now in America, in terms of say
Christianity and government are anything but
what their founders intended.

Luckily, things are not totally out of
control. We don't have anarchy in the streets.

There is help out there. Some folks working
to maintain the moral order.

Not along the lines of Dr. Phil.

More so along North Greenwood Avenue in
Tulsa, Oklahoma.

We're not in Kansas anymore.

... "Is this the bible belt?"

"The buckle."

That's me asking another dumb question, this time at the Tulsa Peace House.

Joni and Timbre Wolf respond together politely.

Yesterday I drove from St. Joseph, Missouri to Tulsa, Oklahoma to speak.

This afternoon I am sitting in a hotel in Fort Worth, watching college basketball on the television. I spent the morning on the back roads.

It was warm on Tuesday when I was in Oklahoma, about 62 degrees. It was one below the morning before in Iowa.

I thought I had never been to Oklahoma, but I do remember something now about a few days in the 1980s spent at El Reno Federal Prison. I think it was during the time of riots at the state prison at McAlester. I remember being glad about the rioting, somebody fighting back. It's easy to hate when you are inside a prison bus wearing handcuffs and shackles.

Sometimes I think I hate America to this very day.

I see what we do and don't do.

But on a long drive like this I realize I don't hate as much as maybe I thought I did.

On the first half of the tour I took the Interstate, whizzing, fighting traffic, and it kind of got to me — by the end of the trip I was ready to fight if somebody in front of me didn't react to the green light like a Formula I drag racer.

This time, when I can, I think I'll take the blue highways, as William Least Heat Moon called them.

And so I got to drive through Coffeyville, Kansas. And I have now seen my first armadillo, albeit deader than shit.

I have been to Bowlegs, Oklahoma now, and seen some of the Sac and Fox, Cherokee and Seminole people, land, casinos — whatever was close to the road. I also passed by Prague, Oklahoma and the Czech Car Wash. I thought for a moment about stopping and saying hello to "my people."

And I have now driven past the sign for Osawatomie, Kansas, where John Brown took the slavery issue into his own hands, or rather at Pottawatomie Creek. Some say he started the Civil War, some say he was a hero, some say he was the first American terrorist.

And there was the sign outside the Highway Baptist Church, near Seminole.

"Will The Road You Are On Get You To God?"

That's a good question. I was driving and did not have a chance to really read the map, so I really don't know. Have you seen the film "*Zeitgeist?*"

Along the way to Tulsa I saw the tops of all the trees bent and broken, for miles and miles. I thought it was a tornado, a big-ass tornado, but I guess it was The Ice Storm of December 2007.

You know, I did a few of these book tour "events" with last year's eastern swing, but this was the first one this year, and it's hard to get going again. It's just weird to see signs set up with your name and to have people take time from their day to come listen to you.

At home there are no signs that say "*Welcome Allen T. Alyan, Author & Activist.*"

But I start in, get back to work, start shaking hands and meeting the people. They are mostly old friends and they welcome me into their circle, tell me about their lives, past and present.

And I remember why I am there. It is for them. Not for me.

That's true, and that's the way it should be, although in the end I get more out of it than they do.

I got to meet "B" and Huti and Jean and Joni and Timbrewolf and Brian and Gary and others. I hear them discuss intently their campaigns against high school military recruitment and depleted uranium and global warming.

Timbrewolf is a big man with long, graying hair. He was a music composition major at the University of Oklahoma years ago and used to be in a band called "*The People's Glorious Five-Year Plan*."

Huti is part Cherokee, and was in the Navy, and also worked in electronics in Silicon Valley, where he once worked on a project to provide "offensive weapons" for the Saudi government. "They said it was defensive, but we knew it wasn't."

Jean and Huti live in Muskogee. Jean has her white car plastered in bumper stickers, putting mine to shame. She is a registered nurse and often stands on street corners dressed in a polar bear costume to draw attention to global warming. She has been interviewed on National Public Radio, *All Things Considered,* within her polar bear capacity.

Joni got arrested at a few local protests, along with Huti and Jean, during visits by Cheney and Bush. Joni fought her conviction and was found not guilty by the necessity defense. That's a big deal.

We went out to eat at China Buffet after-wards. The talk was about politics, about Obama and Hillary, locals like Senator James Inhofe, whom these folks despise, and his challenger,

whom they love. They refer to Kucinich as
"Dennis."

Joni is the organizer for the local Green
Party and talks about a recent visit from Green
Party Presidential candidate Cynthia McKinney.

As always, I know waaay less about the
issues than my hosts. It's ... well ...
disappointing to always, always be the stupid
honored guest, but I am growing used to it.

Afterwards we take a drive around town.
Tulsa is much bigger than I thought.

We stop at the praying hands at the entrance
to Oral Roberts University — two gigantic paws
in sculpture. We stop and everyone looks up,
straining to take it all in out the window.

Huti wonders out loud how much money it
would take to open up the hands.

For those of you who have negative thoughts
about the Bible Belt, about the state of our
nation, of Christianity, about what passes for
theological discourse in this country at this
time, take heart.

You can rejoice in knowing that there is a
strong, small group of people in Tulsa who also
do not buy the bullshit, the propaganda.

They get it.

They are there, on the ground, fighting
every day for this country.

They are the ones we owe our freedom to.
That is what I believe. That is what the book
Cost of Freedom is all about.

That is what this tour is all about.

seeya

— Allen

Note:
Get bread, milk, gum. Kill the little bastards.

[chapter thirty-one]

Good-bye to my Juan, good-bye Rosalita
Adios mis amigos, Jesus y Maria
You won't have a name when you ride the
big air-plane
And all they will call you will be
deportees.

Some of us are illegal, and others not
wanted
Our work contract's out and we have to
move on
But it's six hundred miles to that
Mexican border
They chase us like outlaws, like
rustlers, like thieves.

We died in your hills, we died in your
deserts
We died in your valleys and died on your
plains
We died 'neath your trees and we died in
your bushes
Both sides of the river, we died just
the same.

A sky plane caught fire over Los Gatos
canyon
Like a fireball of lightning, it shook
all our hills
Who are all these friends, all scattered
like dry leaves
The radio says they are just deportees.

    — Woody Guthrie, "Deportees"

WEATHERFORD, TEXAS — I had hoped to make it to Stephenville tonight, but it's midnight, and I'm about an hour or more short. Stephenville is where there have been a recent rash of UFO sightings.

I'll go outside and smoke a cigarette and look around. It's the best I can do. I'm here UFOs, abduct me.

Thursday night I met with the Dallas-Fort Worth 911 Truth group at Crystal's Pizza.

Daniel and Dale are from Dallas. They are jailers in the Dallas County Jail. I mention the old jail and it being in Dealey Plaza and how some inmates said they saw a shooter in the sixth floor window.

Daniel says it's closed now, but they used to hold hangings on the roof. He says former inmates of the jail and older jailers say it's haunted because of that.

Dale is big and bald and he'll be twenty-one soon. He's from Arizona and his dream would be to get onto the Dallas police force and then become a resource officer in the schools.

This morning I went to Mecca. I don't think being in Bethlehem could be any more awe inspiring than where I was today. Maybe a John Prine concert.

Dealey Plaza. 411 Elm Street.

The first day I walked into kindergarten at Lincoln School, Miss Steele had written all

across the blackboard in big fluffy yellow
teacher handwriting, President John F. Kennedy.

In third grade, just after lunch, Sister
Ellen floated into the classroom on the
invisible nun conveyor belt — you couldn't see
their feet — and told us the President had been
shot and that he was dead.

"Why?" I ask Mike Brown, who is standing on
the Grassy Knoll, why he comes here.

"For the truth," says Mike. He is a big,
black man wearing black work clothes. He's got
a deep voice and he's giving folks the
alternative view of history, the op-ed of what
they have just heard nearby in the JFK Museum
tour.

Mike was thirteen in 1963. He shows a color
photo of him in the crowd on Elm Street, a
skinny kid in a red and white checkered shirt,
wide eyes, leaning forward to see the oncoming
motorcade in front of the Dal-Tex building. He
later testified in front of the Warren
Commission when it came to Dallas.

He has been coming to this place ever since
to tell the truth.

What is the truth?

"Everybody ran here," he says, meaning the
Grassy Knoll. "You could smell the gunpowder.
He didn't see any shooters when he arrived, but
he pulls out a black and white photo of a man
in a suit and a white cowboy hat, behind the

fence, carrying something under a jacket or cover that Mike says is a rifle.

There is a police officer in the photo. Mike knows him, shows the two together in a recent color photo. The police officer says the man told him he was with the Secret Service and should keep the crowd that was coming up to the fence area away, which the officer then did. The man disappeared.

It's small. Tiny. So much in so little space. It's like finding out WWII actually took place in a closet. The shot from the Grassy Knoll was close. There is an "X" in the middle lane of the road.

The road angles downward. The Grassy Knoll fence is still there. Right there is where the car disappeared into history with Jackie Kennedy climbing onto the back of the vehicle to retrieve part of her husband's brain.

I walk around to look over. I would be too short to be a shooter, but you realize that the shot was very short. It's all just right there.

The train whistle blows. Behind, there are the tracks, the overpass.

Mike says it's all just as it was then, the fence is the same. He points to the perch where Abraham Zapruder stood with his camera. It's right there, just a few feet away.

This hasn't all been a dream. It's real.

On the back of the fence people have written their names, dedications to the president.

"St. John Hunt was here, son of E. Howard Hunt, 1/13/08."

"JFK, God Bless You."

"George Bush Did It/911 Truth."

Inside the museum they give you headphones and you go up the elevator to the sixth floor. You walk around the parts of the exhibit listening to the audio tour. You learn about the Kennedy presidency, and also about the mood in Dallas before his visit, during his visit.

You see amateur film of the event, still-photos. The crowds were ten-deep along Main Street.

You look out those windows on the sixth floor, down Houston Street where the motorcade came before turning sharply left. There are people all around the area, taking photos, pointing toward the sixth floor, a group gathered out on the Grassy Knoll.

New carpeting, new shiny displays, but the wooden beams and big steel braces are the same. You can touch them, lean against them, feel them.

It's family history, genealogy. We want to know where we came from. It's not like going to see some World War I battlefield. It's now.

There are people alive now who know the truth, who were there. It's a cold, open case. On the timeline of world history it's still the same day.

It's mostly quiet in the museum because people are walking around with earphones, listening to the audio tour. But it's also quiet from intensity, like folks are walking in to view the body of a close friend. When they actually get there it's perhaps more than they can handle.

I had meant to walk around in the neighborhood behind the depository where Oswald ran or walked to get away, but in the tour I learned that he walked out the front door, took a bus, then a transfer, then a cab, then walked, to get home in the Oak Cliff neighbor-hood, change clothes, get his gun, then supposedly kill officer J.D. Tippit, then try to hide in the Texas Theater on Jefferson Boulevard, where he was captured by the Dallas police.

Mike points back over the trees to the double McDonald's arches in the distance and says that's where Kennedy was supposed to be going to speak at a luncheon at the Market Hall. He was just a few minutes from there.

I ask why Oswald ran. Mike says he didn't run, he just went home, to get his gun. Tippit was supposed to kill him. Oswald was the patsy. Maybe he realized at that moment what was happening to him.

Oswald sounds calm on the earphones saying he didn't kill anybody. You stand there, in the spot, and hear those words, and I can't see myself being that cool.

I get lost leaving the area as a matter of course, go along an overpass and find myself in Oak Cliff.

This is where Oswald lived, where Tippit was shot, where the theatre is. It's now a black neighborhood. I'll bet it was white middle class back then.

I make a wrong turn and almost hit a white car. The woman screams and honks. I mouth "sorry" and head back toward downtown.

Mike says that Tippit was supposed to kill Oswald the patsy and that Ruby had to be called in to clean up the job. But who shot Tippit then? And why?

I can't help but wonder what it would have been like to be Oswald at that time, to be boarding that bus, running, with all this happening around him, walking along a normal city street knowing his life would never be okay ever again.

Well, I go all the way through the downtown along Commerce, finally find Main Street and realize this is the motorcade route and will take me back to Dealey Plaza.

Here it is. I pass the spot where Mike stood in 1963.

Here I go, down the dip.

There is Mike on the Grassy Knoll with another group, pointing up to the Dal-Tex rooftop, where he says one of the shooters was, along with two behind the fence and one more on the sixth floor.

"Not Oswald."

Mike has never left Dealey Plaza. He never will.

I'm exiting soon, with President John F. Kennedy still etched into my brain in flaky yellow chalk.

And then — boom — there I am, on the "X". The knoll is right there. There's the overpass.

I turn right to take 35-E.

In a few moments I pass Market Hall, where Kennedy was supposed to speak at a luncheon, then a few moments later the exit for Love Airfield, where the Kennedys landed just before noon and where they left later in the day with the president's body in a box.

— Allen

[chapter thirty-two]

We are living in the future
I'll tell you how I know
I read it in the paper
Fifteen years ago.
We're all driving rocket ships
And talking with our minds
And wearing turquoise jewelry
And standing in soup lines
We are standing in soup lines.

— John Prine, *We Are Living In The Future*

AUSTIN, TEXAS — "Move, you idiot!"

It's happening. Life on these interstate racetracks is getting to me.

I read the bumper sticker on the maroon van.

Jak Se Mas.

"Jake-see-moss?"

"What kind of g.d. thing is that? Indonesian? Move! You Sampan-driving, Tibetan, Waco Turban Cowboy."

I pass on the left, look out the corner of my eye, "Jak Se Mas."

"Yaksay Mash."

It's Czech. My people. Hello in Czech.

I wave and smile.

We recognize each other. Hi. Hi.

We are idiots. My people are idiots.

Yesterday I was in Stephenville, got gas, asked about the guy who saw the UFOs. The girl says he lives in Selden and points the way I'm going.

Selden. And I live in Sheldon.

A sign.

At the sign, with all the inhabitants also listed on the sign, I turn left.

I wave at a guy in his driveway, sitting and reading. I turn around in the church lot and come up behind the guy. He waves backward. He already knows I'm there. I ask about the other guy, who saw the UFOs.

He acts as though he is used to being asked, then directs me to the hill, turn right at the church.

There are several houses, farms, ranches, spreads on the road. I pick out three that have dogs, many dogs, and I decide not to get out. I pick one with no dog and the couple comes out, smiling, used to being asked the question, and point me up to Mike Odom's place.

Up on another hill.

I go up there, down the long lane. More dogs, but one is tied and the others are in the kennel.

I knock and knock. Nobody around.

Back in January it was reported worldwide that right here, in this backyard with the scrub and the hot tub and the children's toys and the sitting chairs, at about six in the evening, Mike Odom, Steve Allen and Lance Jones saw something big in the sky, perhaps a mile long and a half-mile wide.

It headed toward Stephenville, then ten minutes later, it headed back, like a little brother sent to town for smokes.

I wish I could have talked to Mike. But just standing here with the dogs tied up is pretty good too.

On my way out of town I wave at the guy in the chair in his driveway. He waves back.

I also stopped at Mt. Carmel, outside of Waco.

Remember the Branch Davidians?

To me this is holy ground. I don't care what those people believed, that's not what's important to me.

But I feel a connection. I saw these build-ings burn on TV back in 1993. Rosey and I were operating the *Byron Review*, a small newspaper in a small town in southeast Minnesota.

It wasn't too long after I had gotten out of jail for protesting against the U.S. military.

I guess that being in prison, encountering Americans in their courts and justice system, their military, you come to understand that this is not really "the land of the free and the home of the brave."

We all saw it, the flames, nobody coming out of the buildings.

They all burned. We burned them. Our government, our FBI, our ATF.

Later there was a trial. But it was not the FBI on trial, it was the surviving church group members, guilty of not being burned alive.

This place is not a national monument. There is no large sign, no camper parking facilities, no gift shop. There are no smiling families with arms around each other's waists asking Oriental strangers to take their photo with the big mountain in the background.

But it should be. You have to want to find this place, on the Double EE Ranch Road, way out in the country.

There are three of us standing here. Right at our feet is the burned, buried bus, the underground passageway, the underground storm shelter.

You can touch it. It is not glassed-in, not guarded, no surveillance cameras, no mainte-nance man waiting nearby to wipe up any mess you might leave behind.

There are gold fish in the water in the remains.

Right here eighty-two people died, eighteen under the age of ten. Standing right here you can see their charred bodies, while America stands a few feet away, with guns, and the rest of us sat in front of television sets, watching.

At the entrance to the land there are gravestones for each of the eighty-two.

... "Theresa Nobregg, age 19; Gregory A. Summers, age 19; Vanessa Henry, age 19; Raymond Friesen, age 77; Mayanah Schneider, age 2; Melissa Morrison, age 6; Lorraine Sylvia, age 40. ...

Each of the stones has the same day of death: April 19, 1993.

It says that for fifty-one days these people were able to hold off the United States.

I think this is really America.

This is where tourists should go, along with Ruby Ridge, the motel in Memphis, the Ambassador Hotel, the Jumping Bull Compound.

To hell with Mount Rushmore.

It's a long way to Amarillo. If I get there, then maybe I'll see ya.

— Allen

[chapter thirty-three]

When the Earth is sick, the animals will
begin to disappear, when that happens,
The Warriors of the Rainbow will come to
save them.

    – Chief Seattle

DOUGLAS, ARIZONA — "Manuel Escandon
Morales!"

"Presente!"

Tuesday I took part in a ceremony in
downtown Douglas.

Local activists and visiting students from
Buena Vista University in Storm Lake, Iowa,
near my home town of Sheldon, Iowa, were also
there on alternative spring break.

We each hold our cross in the air and the
rest say "Presente!"

On the white cross I hold it says that
Manuel was born Feb. 15, 1967.

He died June 26, 2002 in the desert of
Cochise County, outside of Douglas.

We stand on the Pan American Highway, which
runs from Douglas into Agua Prieta, Mexico.

When we are done the road is lined with
white crosses.

The crosses run from the border patrol port
of entry down the road to the intersection at
the fast food restaurant.

I'm staying with Paul and Judy Plank. They
live about a half hour from me in Iowa, in
Remsen.

During the past ten winters they have been
coming to Arizona. They live in the Arizona
Friends Community outside of Douglas.

Each week the Planks attend the Tuesday
vigils, organized by the local group Healing
Our Borders. Judy is also involved in many
other local projects to help the migrants,
providing work, blankets encouragement.

This is what we should all be doing.

But we are not.

We spent $25 million for a new Border Patrol
station at Douglas. There is lots of money,
lots of jobs in keeping other people poor.
There are all kinds of high-tech cameras and
sensing devices set up all around in the
desert.

We are on a tour of the area and out to look
at the twelve-foot-tall fence. A border patrol
agent sits in a green and white jeep.

As we leave another agent comes up for the 3
p.m. shift change — to watch the fence, in case
some poor people decide to risk their lives to

make a better life for their children, we will be there to make sure they go to jail.

The real terrorists are George Bush & Co. They did 911. That is whom we have to fear, not Manuel Morales.

I am for open borders.

I think, since we are a Christian nation, that we should help poor people. That's kind of what Christianity is all about. I ask Paul and Judy if anyone in their group would agree with me.

"Oh, yes!" they both say.

Paul and Judy will head back to Iowa in about three weeks, to see family and to escape rattlesnake season in the desert. Judy once had to chase one away from her porch with a broom.

I ask about the cactus, the plants, the trees, everything.

"Mesquite, Yucca."

Paul adds a note about tarantulas and scorpions. Killer bees.

"There's nothing warm and cuddly here," says Paul. "Everything is either hard, prickly, or poking."

On Highway 80 into Douglas I passed the "Geronimo Surrenders" monument.

I look around and realize this is where Geronimo was. He's not here anymore. We killed him.

Judy notes that once a year they go over to Agua Prieta to "Revolution Days" where all the children dress up with mustaches and big hats to look like Pancho Villa.

Cool.

He was later killed too, by an assassin to gain a United States reward.

A few days earlier Judy went with friends to Fort Huachuca, one of the places where our military interrogators are trained, such as the ones at Abu Ghraib. The fort is also the place where the Buffalo Soldiers were stationed, the ones who slaughtered the Indians.

In the morning we watch the Winter Soldiers hearings on Democracy Now. Paul and Judy have a grandson serving in Iraq.

Everyone should have seen those hearings.

Why didn't that happen?

One former soldier states:

"This country's apathy. Our president's continued rhetoric. You are all responsible."

He then ripped up the medals General Petraeus had pinned on him.

If that were on NBC, that would be the end of the war.

Another mother and father talk about how their son came to kill himself after coming back from five months in Iraq.

Ever wonder if you're on the wrong side of the fence?

I do.

seeya

— Allen

[chapter thirty-four]

The core basis of our focus is the fact
that humans are going to have to learn
to contact these non-human beings in a
peaceful way. Unfortunately the
political structures have not dealt with
the issue and the covert programs are
military and hardly diplomatic. I mean
they are actually increasingly hostile.

So what we are doing is a citizens
diplomacy effort and we have laid down
protocols that are interrelated and very
spiritually based and we believe that we
are spiritually conscious beings and
there is a mind of the cosmos that
shines in every being.

> – Dr. Steven Greer, *The Disclosure
> Project*

We always said whoever feels worse about
missing the others, get in touch.

Of course, we never did.

It was a lot of years later that I came back
to town.

I didn't have the Chevy anymore. We had a
blue Toyota, no rust, a dent in the right rear
wheel well. I don't know the year or brand.

I came in on 17 past the sign for the steel
mill, The Lonely Bull, Prairie Park. Turned

right on state hospital road, past the state
hospital, past the community college.

I drove past the new "Y" and stopped at the
intersection of a new McDonald's, the old
Godfather's, and a liquor store one of the guys
owns. I turned left toward the high school.

You know those guys who go away to be monks?

They say they don't do it to get away from
the world. They say they are more fully engaged
with the world, more truly involved with the
world by spending all their days behind a brick
wall.

They have to say that. Or maybe they really
think that, or maybe it's written down in some
brown book as something they have to say if
somebody asks.

But I think it's pretty clear that the
reason you would go away to be a monk would be
to escape, to get away. You would have to be
the kind of guy who would just love to run away
and never stop running, who would think sitting
in a dark, quiet room with a hood over your
head and some warm goat tea close by, with some
brother monk down the hall and around the
corner playing hymns on a comb would be like
being drunk all day long.

The monk brochures say they would be just as
comfortable teaching sophomore math or selling

money at state bank or selling feed or hanging
from their toes cleaning windows. Wouldn't
matter to them. They choose to be alone all day
in order to more fully encounter the world.

Of course, nobody understands that and so it
sounds about right.

But it's total bullshit. It has to be.

Right?

That's why I'm in town, to be a monk.

I kept going, past the post office, library,
railroad tracks, radio station, the old motel
downtown.

I pulled up to the stop light at Main. It's
actually called New Field Avenue.

Wow.

I gawked like I was in the big city.

There was a boulevard thing in the middle.

A Mexican couple pushed a stroller across
the street in front of me.

The big bank on the corner was a furniture
store, or it was, or it was going to be.

The old "Y", where we used to sit with our
girlfriends in the cushion chairs in the big
lobby or play Stratego in the game room or swim

or play basketball, was now a parking lot for a
new bank, which used to be a huge post office,
where I signed up three months late for the
draft.

I drove all the way down Main, slow, like an
old guy in the country checking his neighbors'
fields.

Well, I don't know why, but I went out to
the state hospital.

I didn't go just there. I was out driving
all over to see what had changed.

It was pretty interesting. Every street had
a memory.

I drove around the half circle slow 'cause
there's speed bumps.

Actually I do know why I went out there.
Lotsa reasons.

I stared at each building because for one
reason I had an uncle who's supposed to have
been in there and he died in there.

I didn't find out 'til after he was dead. I
called out there and asked about him and they
said they couldn't tell me if he was ever there
or not.

And because I heard that the place was
really a concentration camp, not for Germans

and Japs, but Americans. I don't know who told me that stuff, or how I got it, but somehow I heard it, somewhere.

And I always wondered about that one guy I saw on the school tour, the guy who showed me how to get cow tit.

The whole circle was full of huge buildings, big brick buildings.

Some had plyboard over the front doors. Some windows were busted.

No people.

I came to the end of the circle drive and the last building, smaller than the rest, the runt, had a snow fence marking the front yard. A homemade sign by the front doors said they rented rooms for $39.95.

He was right there.

Sitting on the ledge of the steps.

He looked like he could be smoking.

He stared at me. He wore a stocking cap on a tilt. The old Norse fisherman, just like he did all those years ago.

I remember because it was Christmas time and we had seen *Captains Courageous* in the gym for our present from the sisters. And then we went out to the hospital for our tour for the rest of the day.

I thought the guy who called me over to milk was the same guy as the one in the movie, so at the time I got a little scared, wondering what was real and not.

I pulled the Toyota into a parking spot.

He kept looking at me.

Maybe he recognized I was the kid from the tour.

I got out and started walking around looking for a door in the fence.

He pointed with the hand with the cigarette toward the gate.

I walked over.

You don't know me, I said.

He shook his head.

He was old. So was I.

I introduced myself and said I was the kid from the Christmas school tour.

He said he recalled quite a few kids coming through when he was working in the dairy.

"We used to have a Holstein herd here, a couple of beautiful Brown Swiss, too. Had milk and cheese for all the prisoners, staff, what have you."

Prisoners? I said. Or I thought it. Maybe I didn't say anything.

I asked if he knew my uncle. He said, probably.

"There were so many guys going through here it's hard to say. But I knew most of 'em, because of the dairy. I took milk to all the units, had my own deals going for cigarettes. You get by how you are able."

He said the men in the New Field State Hospital were not insane.

"Least when they came in," he said. "That's what they wanted you and all the others to think."

He was small, smaller than he was, I figured. But his hands were large and thick like his leather boots, re-stitched and patched and muscular. He crossed his legs easily and smoked.

The tanned face under the pitched blue cap like it was built that way, the sharp nose like the prow of a ship cutting through the bullshit days, the hair still deep-black.

I sat across from him and mostly listened.

He said this building was a work release center for a while after the state hospital closed up. Then the city or county took it over and turned it into apartments.

He was from New Field, south side.

"With all us Indians."

His name was Christian Jump Cornfield.

"You can call me Vince."

He left New Field High School during his junior year.

"I enlisted."

He went to the war, got shot, came back and started writing letters to the editor, to the Army, to the governor, the president.

"They arrested me, charged me with being a drunk Indian, put me in county, then out here."

He said he was put into isolation for what might have been years. He claimed he was tortured.

"Lots of guys were medicated," he said. "They slept away years."

Vince said he was the guy who wrote the Fuck You on the bridge.

My face must have lit up like a real Christmas tree in the living room the day after Thanksgiving.

"Really?"

He said he got out of his window one night
and was going to escape. He got as far as the
bridge.

"Pretty far," he said, nodding his head at
the smoke in his hand.

There were flashing lights coming from way
down the road, some farmers coming in pickups
behind him, vigilantes.

"I climbed up on the bridge to get away,
sort of.

"I slipped, hit my face, hard, on the flat
iron. My nose was bleeding like hell.

"I knew it was over. My hands were covered
in the shit.

"With the cops down there watching me with
the lights flashing and their guns drawn on me
I wrote my message on the bridge.

"The police took me back to the state house.
I was smiling wide in the back seat. You can't
get blood off once it's somewhere."

He was released a few months after the war
ended, about the same time the rest of us
graduated.

He lived with his father on the south end,
then an uncle for a while, then went down to

Lincoln for a while, was homeless a lot of the time, in Lancaster County Jail the rest mostly.

He just recently got the room here, along with a sweet job cutting the grass on the grounds.

He rolled another cigarette, then another, and handed one to me.

He puffed and winced and leaned forward.

"That's the secret of life," he said in a coarse throaty growl.

He put his head back and almost laughed, smiling wide with his eyes, and mouth, and nose.

"Don't you white guys come to old Indians for that?" he said.

"The big secret?

"Fuck you," he said. "It's the Ying to the Yes-Sir Yang.

"Ghandi knew it. Julia Child knew it."

He puffed and winced and flicked into a pants cuff.

"Martin King knew it. Sitting Bull.

"Dorothy Day.

"Chinga tu madre, if you're Mexican.

"Chinka-chink-ching, if you're Chinese.

"But you have to say it in American, right?"

I nodded.

"The bridge, that's where you can say all sorts of things, things you can't say anywhere else," he said. "Like in that one dancing show from the '90s, '80s?

"I knew what I was doing, where I was going," he leaned in again, close, like the trees or empty buildings could hear, like the lonely widows in the houses across the highway were watching.

"I was going to the bridge.

"Your alien knew it too.

"That's why he was climbing up there, I'll bet.

"People tell you to sit up straight, drive on the right side of the road.

"If you do it, you die.

"If you fight, they kill you, right?

"So, those are the choices.

"Die. Get killed.

"Living is not one of the choices. None of the above.

"Unless you say F.U."

Way down on Fifteenth Street there was this big new stop light. I turned left on the green arrow, headed south, past Johnny Carson's childhood home, checking every car, with my hand on top of the steering wheel ready to wave.

Before, I could tell you everyone who was out with one round.

I didn't recognize any of these people.

I stopped at three more lights that didn't used to be there.

I looked at the pictures on the billboards of insurance agents.

I looked for a phone booth with a book, or just a booth.

I could try the bar out in the strip mall by Gibson's. I suppose it wouldn't take that long to walk up and down the new graves. For the past ... that would take forever.

There they were.

I pulled in.

A.C. and Rick were leaning against someone else's new red SUV.

You ever, I don't know, listen to people? And you see they have this second dimension? The ignorant bigot feels lowly because his brother has more money than he does.

And he's not really an ignorant whatever now, he's more. He's got more sides to him, more inches of depth.

That's what I could see right away in A.C. and Rick standing there.

There was more.

I could still recognize them. That's kind of amazing too.

They were different.

Or not.

I got out and leaned on the ol' blue Toyota.

"You never came to the reunions," said A.C.

"I didn't want to."

"Oh."

"How's it goin'?" I said.

"Awesome," said Rick. He reached out to shake my hand. Then I reached over to A.C.

"How's the Huskers?" I asked.

"Don't know," said A.C.

"Overseas bases, gorilla warfare."

I looked at A.C.

"Inter-continental airways."

He stared at me like I was speaking pig-Latin.

We crossed our arms, leaned against the cars and watched traffic. I had to look back over my shoulder or stare at those two.

"Extraterrestrials," Rick mumbled, and I thought, here we go. At least that's what I thought he said.

"Mexicans," he said.

"Way-ass too many. 'Ts what my dad says."

"He must be one thousand years old by now," I said.

"Uh-uh," said Rick.

"Russians, criminals, terrorists, Negroes, space-men. All aliens. Extra-terrestrials. Shouldn't be here. We got enough already. We don't need 'em."

"Go Big Red," said A.C.

"What?" I said.

"Jew hear that one song?" said A.C.

"I don't know," I said.

"You can't say that," said A.C.

"What?" I said.

"What he said before."

"About what?" Rick turned.

"What are you back for?" A.C. asked me.

"Bein' a monk."

"About aliens," said A.C. to Rick.

"A monk?" said Rick.

"What kind of a monk?" said A.C.

"A monk?" said Rick.

"A monk."

"What kind of a monk?" said A.C.

"Just a monk," I said. "You know."

"You can't talk about aliens," A.C. said. "There's no such thing."

We stood there some more, waiting for people to wave and honk so we could wave back. Nobody really did.

"Remember?" I said.

"How could we forget?" said A.C. "Classic. Rosebud."

"Black and white," I said. "No rust."

"Murder," said Rick.

To anyone else it would have seemed like we were speaking Tlingit.

We all knew what was being said.

A.C. was talking about one of the summer
trips to Colorado. After we all quit our summer
construction jobs we drove to Colorado to camp
out in Estes Park, Vail, somewhere, drink Coors
beer.

It was only a long day's drive, but to us we
were each Marco Goddamned Fucking Polo.

I had scars on the insides of both of my
arms, and my chest, from running into a barbed
wire fence. I'd been window peeking on a
trailer while we were camping near Estes.

Rosebud was the old pickup we bought on the
way after my Volkswagen van broke down three
hours from home.

"We on da job," said A.C.

"I found your diary underneath some sod,"
Rick sang, and we all smiled silently about the
summer we worked for the school system and one
of our jobs for a few days was to lay sod some
fucking where.

"We killed a Mexican," said Rick.

You could see the weight coming off his
shoulders like steam, decades of pressure
releasing. He stood straighter.

He looked each of us straight-on through
watery eyes.

"Mexican?" said A.C. "No. It was an Allen, that one kid, Peter Allen. They moved."

I looked at both of them like they had just appeared in front of me on a special cruise to Fatima or some shit.

I jumped up, my knees to my chest.

"What?

"You dumb fucks!

"It was an alien! Outerspace!

"You said!"

I poked Rick in the chest.

The dawn of enlightenment fell down Rick's face like the New Year's Eve ball on TV. First the brow ridge receded, then the mouth closed. The eyes lit brightly.

He pushed me.

"You thought it was a space man?

"You think we shot E.T.!"

He grabbed his knees.

A.C. fell to the concrete, between the two cars.

They laughed. Loud.

I stood there, stuck my hands halfway into my front pockets.

"Twist and chow." A.C. managed to get it out and it sent them both into another wave of paroxysms.

I used to think it was twist and chow, rather than twist and shout. So what? Fuckers.

They pulled themselves up by both vehicles, wiping their eyes with their fists.

"We killed a Mexican?" I got in close to Rick.

"Yeah, ha, geez, I think so."

"We did?"

A.C. roared and pushed Rick back up against the SUV.

"God-dammit!"

A.C. pushed him again.

"Nobody ever said nothing," Rick whispered.

"It was never in the news, the paper."

"You sure?" I said.

"Anybody ever come arrest you?" asked Rick.

"I don't know," he said. "Coulda been kind of a big head. Fu-uck."

"Let's go," I said.

We got into the Toyota.

We headed out on Thirteenth Street toward the viaduct, over the tracks.

"You going to be a monk?" said A.C.

"Yeah," I said. "I guess."

"I don't go to church," he said, and he looked at both of us like we were supposed to say something.

[chapter thirty-five]

I'm in love with the Kum N' Go girl.
Ass't mgr.
Her nametag.
"Kay."
You have a good day.
I will. Now.
Kay. Kay. Kay.
I walk out the door.
Float.

        — A.T.A.

Well, there they were, final-fucking-ly.

I jerked the wheel and cut in front of a
tiny human bus. God.

I jumped the curb. I swerved, this way,
that.

Found a parking spot, actually took up two
spots.

If I backed up, I could maybe straighten it
out.

I decided to just stay put.

They looked at me then continued talking.

They now drove pieces of shit.

I watched them get into a vehicle and drive
away.

I followed them.

They went out to the bridge.

I followed them, from a distance, from behind a van filled with Mexicans, going fifteen miles an hour, which was being followed by a local police cruiser, with a brown and yellow state patrol car beside it in the right lane.

I managed to keep Kenny's Blue Piece Of Shit in sight.

At the light in front of the new Super Wal-Mart I was gawking around and had to slam the brakes to keep from ramming into them.

They turned off the highway and I turned with them.

There were no other cars on the road so I wasn't very inconspicuous. They slowed way down to get me to go around, but I stuck with them.

They speeded up. I went faster.

Then I slowed a little, trying to get them to forget about me.

Kenny took the left turn onto the gravel road to the bridge.

I never told you — well, I did, but it was a lie, which is another Type-A trait. I'm not sure where it came from. I try to fight it, but it's like the V's and their cheeseburgers, you win some and you lose some. It's a constant battle.

Anyway, about the C's, the really, really secret life of C's.

They don't come to earth because they are Earthophiles.

Actually they are Earthophobes, to the max.

They hate everything human.

They are hillbillys who sit around in the woods twanging on their wickbows, blowing their roogledeeoohs, talking about humans, and how they own the universe, run everything, for themselves, and on and on, it goes, generation to generation.

But it's true they don't drive. Not can't, won't.

And I was driving the bus.

They pay a good price for a special trip. We can't allow weapons, but we do look the other way regarding a certain amount of harassment, good fun, letting steam off.

And so Carl was howling, saying FU to the earthlings in the car. And he was climbing up there on the bridge, like an Indian warrior showing how brave he was by riding right up to the soldier and touching him with his stick, counting coup.

And they shot him.

The little bastards.

Kenny and Rick and A.C. drove along the old gravel road headed toward Broken Bridge.

Kenny glided to a stop about fifty yards from the new concrete overpass, the same spot where he had stopped so many years before when Rick got out to shoot Carl.

Allen pulled up right behind, almost touching Kenny's bumper.

"What thuf ... ?" Rick turned to glare out the back window.

He got out and met Allen already walking up.

"Hey!" Rick said. "You!"

Allen smiled.

A.C. was now sitting in his window.

Kenny had his door open and was standing, watching Allen and Rick, with one arm over the door and one on the car roof, one foot up inside the car, the other on the ground.

"That bridge used to be different," Allen said.

"What?" said Rick.

They all looked back at the new concrete bridge.

"Yeah," said A.C.

"That sucks," Kenny said.

"I liked the old one," Allen said. "Rustic, more real."

"Big iron thing," said Kenny.

"Creepy," said Rick. "This is better. I didn't know they did this."

Allen walked around Rick, and stood next to Kenny. They all stared at the new, flat concrete bridge, concrete road, with low, concrete sides.

"We used to write on the old one," said Allen.

"We?" Rick came up to stand behind Allen and Kenny.

A.C. climbed out of his window to sit on the roof, his feet on the window. Kenny glanced at him, then back at the bridge.

"What's your name?" said Kenny.

"Allen. Al Alyan."

He reached up to shake Kenny's hand.

Kenny looked at him, then came around the open door to shake.

Allen reached out to Rick. Rick looked away, over Allen's shoulder, at the bridge.

"Who's we?" said Rick.

"You from Battle Ground?" said A.C. "Towntonville?

"No," Allen smiled. "Not really."

"You're not from around here, are you?" said Rick with a snarl.

Allen looked back, over his shoulder to Rick.

"Fuck you," Allen said.

Rick shot his eyes to Allen.

Kenny started to move to step between them.

A.C. scooted over to the edge of the roof to look down on them.

Allen had his hands in his front pockets. He kept them there as Rick stepped up.

"Dude," said Allen. "The bridge. It used to have writing on it, remember?"

"Fuck you!" said A.C., hell-ya."

"How do you know?" said Rick.

Kenny pushed between them to get free and started to walk up toward the bridge and the river.

Allen followed, then Rick.

A.C. watched them for a while, then slid down the windshield, over the hood, onto the ground.

They all stopped together at the edge of the gravel.

"Right there," Allen pointed up to where the iron railings and the Fuck You would have been.

"It said Fuck You," said A.C. from behind. "That was so great."

Allen looked back and said, "It really was. It's the secret of life."

"Right," said Rick, smiling.

"How do you know?" Kenny turned to look squarely on Allen.

For a moment everyone looked squarely on every one else, back and forth, square in the eyes, turning squarely to face each other, shoulder to shoulder, inquisitive looks cast every which way, glances like light sabers in the bright Nebraska afternoon sun.

"Christian ... Jump ... Cornfield," said Kenny, slowly, carefully, not wanting to say something stupid.

"Vince!" smiled Allen.

"He's a C, like Carl. He defected."

"What?" said Kenny.

"Carl?" said A.C.

"Who's Carl," said Kenny.

"Christian Jump what?" said Rick.

"He's the guy who wrote the Fuck You," said Kenny. "Didn't I tell you? I meant to tell you. Maybe I didn't."

"You never told us," said A.C.

"I went out to see him, at the state hospital."

"Who the fuck is he?" said Rick.

"Who the fuck is Carl?" said A.C.

"Who the fuck are *you*?" Rick looked at Allen.

Allen stepped back and turned to approach the bridge, slowly, keeping his hands in his pockets, kicking up contemplative Buddhist cowboy dust.

He stopped at the side of the bridge, facing the water. The others filled in around him.

A pheasant cackle was followed by a resigned moo.

The water dribbled. A breeze pushed through the trees.

"I was here that night," said Allen.

"What night?" said A.C.

"You know, that night," said Allen, staring ahead.

"In the hippie bus," said Rick.

"We should have rammed him," he looked at Kenny and gritted his teeth. He reached to grab Allen.

Kenny grabbed Rick's arm in mid-air.

Allen, his hands in his pockets, stared straight.

"He's buried right out there."

"Who thuf ... ?" gasped A.C.

"You know who," said Allen.

"Carl?" said Kenny, dropping Rick's arm.

Allen nodded his head.

"Carl."

"Carl," said Kenny. "A friend of yours?"

Allen shook his head.

"A customer."

He looked down and out the side of his eyes toward Rick.

"I'm *not* from around here."

"Geezuz," A.C. took a step back.

"Why is Carl buried ... out there?" said Kenny.

"How do you know Christian Cornfield?"

Allen smiled.

"I'm not crazy," he said. "I've never been a patient, a prisoner, at your state hospital."

He pointed above the trees, on the other side of the little over-run swamp.

"Right there. That's where I was sitting, in my bus — my *Magic School Bus*."

Allen glanced around the group for understanding, landing on Kenny.

"I have developed this habit of dropping cultural references far too often. Without appearing too hyper-introspective, I think it's part of trying to fit in."

Kenny nodded.

"You would not believe, or maybe you would, the number of times I have been able to work Jefferson Starship, Jefferson Airplane, and 'Beam Me Up Scottie' into the conversation. Not to mention, 'You've never heard of the Millennium Falcon? It's the ship that made the Kessel run in less than 12 parsecs.'"

He turned to look squarely into Rick's eyes.

"My spaceship."

"God-damn!" A.C. took off to run. He skidded to a smoky stop after three steps and stayed there.

Kenny took one slow motion step backward.

Rick stared Allen right in his alien motherfucker eyes.

"There was a drawing," said Allen, locked in ojo y ojo combat with Rick. "A stick drawing, an alien stereotype, pointing at the FU."

A.C. slowly walked back to them.

"I put it there."

"Holy shit!" A.C. fell to the ground and crawled into the ditch, then lay there watching the others.

"In honor of the one you murdered. Fuck You is their way, their code, their motto, their raison d'etre, their ... "

"Stop!" said Kenny. "We got it! Fuck you!"

"So clear, so American, so you. Also, so indelibly 'C.'"

"Fuck," said Rick.

"I've come to kill you," said Allen.

"Oh, God," said A.C.

"Or not."

"Why did you bury Carl here?" said A.C. from the weeds.

"I'm conflicted. You are murderers, cowards, cretins. You treat others, those unlike you and the creatures of your earth — and the very earth itself — with complete disdain. The only thing that matters is you, you, you.

"And yet ... and yet there are those among you ... "

He looked at Kenny.

"Who are contemplating being monks, thinking about trying to figure things out, to do something with their life, to ... "

"Please. Dude." Kenny put up one hand and shook his head.

"Kind-of-an-ET-heart-thing," Allen said quickly.

"You ain't killin' shit, space-man," said Rick.

"Are you going to kill us?" said A.C.

"I s'pose you've got a fucking ray gun," said Rick.

Allen looked squarely into Rick's quizzical gaze.

"No," said Allen. "I'd just beat the shit out of you.

"I've been thinking about that for a long time," he said.

"Let's walk."

Allen led them down into the ditch, past A.C., along the edge of the bog shit, into the trees.

He stopped at a pile of rocks at the base of a big fucking tree.

"This it?" said Rick.

Allen nodded.

Rick fell to his knees, dropped his head to his chest and sobbed.

"Ohhhh, God ... somebody's gonna to have to pay for this," said Kenny.

"Somebody has," said Allen.

Allen sat.

They formed a semi-circle behind Rick.

They leaned back on the palms of their hands.

Rick sat up, then moved around the little rock headstone, closed his eyes and rested his head against the tree, one arm draped over a bent knee.

"Why did you bury him here?" asked Kenny. "If he didn't like it here."

"He loved it here," said Allen.

"He just didn't like you. None of the C's do. They've been coming here for years. Lots of years, before you were here.

"They say you ruined it here. You are stupid, backward, juvenile, arrogant people. That you ruin everything you touch."

Kenny put up a hand and closed his eyes, to say, we fucking get it, dude.

"And I had other shit to do," said Allen. "This was really just the start of my night. I had more stops to make.

"The other C's didn't want Carl stinking up the whole bus. They said, hey, why not just debrgadrop him right here?

"So I said sure, why not? I'm cool with that."

They sat in the soft shade of the shelter belt, not hearing the little white airplane buzzing overhead, or the tiny coyote pups whining for their mother at the mouth of the den, or the crackling of the corn stalks in the breeze, or ...

"How did you know it was us?" Kenny said. "We don't look the same as we did back then. We look way different."

"Well," said Allen.

"This is true. The answer is that you guys
are so focused on the physical body, when it is
the spiritual that is primary, that is the real
deal. You, we, each have a spiritual finger-
print kind of, an aura ... "

"Odor?" said A.C.

"No," said Allen, "that would be Bigfoot.
Your kind don't stink near as much as you think
you do. You're fine. You should chill."

Allen looked up through the trees to the
sky.

"See anyone you recognize?" Kenny smiled.

Allen grinned.

"No, not really.

"Let me just say this. We can't say
everything today, but this is fucking
important.

"We are all connected, dude. In spirit, if
not in experience or biology, emotions,
knowledge, talents, that stuff.

"You guys really, really need to start to
pull your heads out of your aftefartens.

"Sorry."

"S'ok," said Rick. "Go 'head."

"You need to start to get the universal part of yourself. And then maybe you wouldn't be so afraid of me, of others on your planet who are different, of each other. And then you wouldn't hurt each other. That shit is only because you're afraid. Scared shitless.

"This is a cosmic moment, dude. The dawning of the Age of Aquarius, all that shit, the next stage of human development.

"Or not."

He looked at them, hoping they would get it.

"I guess I shouldn't be a monk then," said Kenny, looking down to scratch the dirt with the heel of his tennis shoe.

"No," Allen looked laser beams into Kenny's eyes.

"No, that's exactly what you should do ... If you want to."

He looked at A.C. and then Rick.

"Don't go to work every day at the same time and take the same route for forty-fucking years, and expect that to do it.

"Because you are in for a big fucking ... a big disappointment."

They sat back on their hands and let time pass in front of their eyes.

Allen said he was going to tell them a story about his past, his human squeeezed-past.

"And I just like Steinbeck. Always have. Even on Los Gatos. He's been there. Great characters, detail, setting, all that. And he's got something to say. Not many can pull that off, or even try."

> Ever see a cock-pheasant, all stiff and beautiful ever' feather drawed and painted, an' even his eyes drawed in pretty? An' bang! You pick him up, bloody and twisted, an' you spoiled somepin better'n you.

"That's John Steinbeck, *The Grapes of Wrath*," Allen said. "My story's about a Ten Point Norwegian."

> Recently six hunters were killed in Wisconsin and another is now headed off to prison for life.
>
> Well, that's a start.
>
> I don't like hunters. They kill when they do not need to. When I see a bunch out in a field in their bright orange dunce caps, I try to honk and then flip them the bird while they raise their shotguns in salute.
>
> I used to be a hunter. My dad took me pheasant hunting in northeast Nebraska back in the '60s. He was from South Dakota and had hunting in his blood. I bought an Ithaca 12-gauge with a ribbed sight, with my own money.

And then I really got hooked on duck hunting somewhere in the '70s. Ducks and geese fascinated me. I think because they came from somewhere else. They were migrating, passing through, when the pheasants and me had only been just here.

Then one day I downed a hen mallard in a slough, cornered her and tried to kill her off by holding her head under water.

I thought to myself, how stupid is this, for one, trying to drown a duck, we could be here all day, and secondly, trying to kill this bird, for what damned reason?

So I let her up. She swam away, to die some day, some way. I walked away, headed toward the same. Threw the Ithaca in the swamp, or sold it, or left it in the trunk of my car. I forget.

I heard that later my high school group of friends would joke about "pre-duck Alyan" and "post-duck Alyan" as later I went on to seminary, civil disobedience, etc. I don't see them anymore, they were so pre-duck.

I was a dumb guy once, probably still am. Dumb guys are the last to know.

I've seen deer hung up in the front yard of somebody's home, in town, while little kids walk past on their way to school. I've seen hunters gloating over dead deer in the field, big brain-dead

grins on their faces. I've heard
measured defenses of hunting from guys
who really should know better.

And I've seen the hunting channel,
really big, really-really dumb guys
whispering, pointing toward the bear or
deer they are about to kill for no
reason. Then later going up and petting
the dead animal like they just loved it
so much they had to kill it.

There is some sick psychology to
hunting, harvesting they call it.

You see something beautiful, majestic,
but just beyond your reach, so you kill
it and there it is, you own it, put it
on your wall and it is yours, like the
Silver Hummer in the drive, or Mary Jane
from the cheerleading squad upstairs
boiling bologna.

And you bathe in the afterglow in your
new basement den, your feet propped up
in just your orange socks, watching
football on a screen the size of
Vermont.

No wonder this country will not last
much longer. That's probably a good
thing.

It's like when God handed out brains,
the line was much longer than he had
anticipated, and after a point, he still
had the whole midwestern United States
to do.

So he said, "Hey, guys, all I've got
left are these orange mittens and these
camouflaged socks, sorry. But they're
pretty cool, right? See, you put them
on, I can't see you! Here. Yeah, that
looks great. No, really."

And the dumb guys scooped up the orange
and camouflaged hats and pants and coats
and said, "Let's git 'r done," with no
idea what that meant.

Over Thanksgiving, my wife, son,
daughter, mother-in-law, and I slumped
toward east-central South Dakota to my
brother-in-law-the-banker's place.

On the way I spotted this enlightened
billboard: "SD Rejects Animal Activists.
Fur, Fish, Livestock Are Are Economy."

Down the road a bit, like Burma-Shave on
a mental hospital front lawn: "The
United States Rejects Human Life
Advocates. Bullets, Bombs, Caskets Are
Are Economy."

I am so proud to be an American.

No, I'm kidding.

A while back there was a photo in the
paper of another Wisconsin hunter, this
one still kickin', who had bagged a 28-
point buck.

Remember the song about the turty-point
buck? No relation.

Well, the hunter says in the article as he holds the animal's antlers for the photographer, while the deer's eyes hang half-closed and the tongue lolls out the side of the mouth, that he really, seriously feels kind of bad about taking such a beautiful creature from the woods.

No, really.

Don't believe it folks.

He is a dumb guy wearing orange clothes with a deer head in his hands.

He'll say anything to stay out of prison.

An' eatin' him don't never make it up to you, 'cause you spoiled somepin in yaself, an' you can't never fix it up.

Though Allen was not sure if they were still awake, he told the others that he might be sticking around for a while.

"That's one of the problems with coming to America, oftentimes after a period of time you are not able to squeeeze. He patted his stomach. You would be surprised at how much the influx to your nation is due to necessity rather than preference.

"However, that's not really all of it, or even most of it. I ... do you know about that song by Alanis, umm, Morissette?

"Thank you, terror. Thank you frailty? You know that?

"It's about being human. The video shows her on the street, in the subway, in the nude, open, vulnerable."

"Naked?" said A.C., looking up at Allen and squinting his eyes at the sun.

"I'd like to learn that.

"From you."

Allen looked into A.C.'s eyes.

He stared into A.C.'s eyes. Allen tried to telepathically impart knowledge to A.C. about the wisdom of Alanis Morissette, a big star on Los Gatos.

A.C. tried telepathically to tell Allen that if he thought he was going to get naked right then, in daylight, right now, he could kiss his ever-lastin' terrestrial butt.

"Are you still going to kill us?" asked A.C., barely keeping his eyes open.

"Fly me away to the bright side of the moon," he muttered a dirge. That's prob'ly how you do it."

Allen looked at A.C.

Allen licked his lips. His eyes went all Chinese Alien and shit.

A.C. thought he caught a glimpse of a long, lizard-like tongue slithering out for just a moment.

Allen sat extremely straight.

"Nah, fuck it, let's go bowling," he said.

Slowly, but inevitably, they all crawled up to stand.

"Are we going to die?" said A.C.

"Can you pay attention for one-fucking moment?" Rick said.

Allen put his arms around A.C. and Rick's shoulders.

Kenny followed behind, stopping to look back, then up, then around, then moving on to catch up.

"Not today," said Allen. "Not today."

..

More Critical Acclaim

Periodically, a new novel by Mike Palecek explodes out of the heartland. Without fail, Palecek's writing is gripping, entertaining, artful and powerfully expresses the crying need for social justice in a broken world. His brand new book is *Speak English* and I can't wait to get my hands on it!

♦ Ray Korona is an activist musician and songwriter

When one begins cranking, *Speak English* plays a back-country tune of rednecks and ETs. And then — surprise! — the lid pops open, and a Jack-in-the-box springs out, sounding very like Mike Palecek, on the road, singing other songs, a voice pleading obvious truths in a culture designed to annihilate them. But when the lid clicks down again, we find that our Mike-in-the-box — alas! — is also an alien doing a thorough tour of humanity.

Hmmm. Problematic. What does that make those of us who identify with him and his perspective? Are we aliens too, extra-terrestrials on this version of the earth? That would explain a lot of things

♦ Marc Estrin is the author of *Insect Dreams, The Education of Arnold Hitler, Golem Songs, The Good Doctor Guillotine*, and more

In *Speak English*, readers will find their favorite Michael Palecek themes (Truth, Justice and Xenophobia) in one of his most successful blends of social critique, humor, outrage and poignancy. In Palecek's work, the hypocrisy of the powers that be — corporate-controlled government, capitalism, institutionalized religion, mainstream consumer culture — is juxtaposed with favorite urban legends. Certainly, government lies are no stranger than, say, Bigfoot, or in this case, Aliens.

In roughly three sections, the first successfully and most entertainingly captures the voice of the clueless Midwestern dude who accidentally provides some flashes of bitingly ironic insight. The second and largest section moves to the author's diary of his actual travels across the United States (Canada refused him entry due to his having been arrested for civil disobedience) as part of a book tour. The real people he meets on this travels — peace and social justice activists, owners of independent bookstores, community builders — offer a counterpoint to the bigoted folks elsewhere in the book. The final portion returns to the original story, but with the narrator in a little more reflective mood. Michael Palecek is becoming a favorite on the "alt-publishing" circuit. This books is a "must read" for Palecek fans, and a great introduction for those who haven't yet discovered him.

♦ Holly Hart, chairs the Iowa Green Party

American culture is not safe. Mike Palecek is amongst us again. You will never look at space aliens, Schlitz beer, old Chevys, hunting, hippies, 9-11, or the sheer insanity of the military/ corporate complex the same again. *Speak English* is a wild ride of hilarity and brilliant social commentary.

A must read if there ever was one. Bravo!

♦ Doug Dralme, poet, is author of *Slaves of the Harvest, Unoccupied Zone,* and *Madmen*

With *Speak English*, Mike Palecek takes us on a journey across a strange but disturbingly familiar American landscape, populated by the people we encounter everyday but never consider twice, and the aliens whose lives we never imagine.

♦ Chris Cook is a contributing editor to *Pacific Free Press* and plays host at *Gorilla Radio*

Centuries ago, before we humans got too damn smart for our own good, a person willing to rise above the herd mentality and focus on the big picture was often labeled a prophet. Unfortunately for Mike Palecek, he's stuck in the age of attention deficit, fiscal quarters, and instant messaging. I'm just saying.

♦ Mickey Z. is a writer and activist

Mike Palecek's latest is weird, funny and totally serious all at the same time. From a mysterious shooting at the beginning to a tour through the U.S. touching on everything from George Bush's involvement with 9-11 and the plot to kill JFK, you won't be able to put *Speak English* down.

◆ Dave Zweifel is editor emeritus for *The Capital Times*, Madison , Wisconsin

I have just visited Mason City, Iowa. Not really. But is there any more authenticity than the midwest through the words of Michael Palecek? America for that matter. Michael Palecek's new novel, *Speak English*, is a pointblank, right on, hit over the head reminder of the Truth about the United States Government and all through the eyes of a passionate, shy, beer drinking alien. If you are truly concerned about what is going on in this country you are probably an alien too and should definitely read *Speak English*.

◆ Nora Nickerson is a Tucson poet and peace activist who is really an alien from Planet N

Palecek takes us on a fast ride through the heartland, downshifting only to signal the curves of the hypocracy of present day U.S. empire. He nails the culture as accurately as he does the throttle. This road trip should raise the hairs on your head and perhaps arouse you from the slumber of high fructose brain fade. Palecek isn't afraid to point out that there are many roads with bad signage, some from sheer neglect, others by cynical intent. Your job is to sort out the right fork to take; the road to truth.

◆ Jim Lynch is a radio host and professional photographer

I know Mike from his politics in which he exhibits passion, great intelligence (mostly because I agree with him) and a profound sensitivity and understanding of the workings of the world these days.

I had no idea that he was such a masterful and brilliant writer/ storyteller. Since I have retired from talk radio, I read a great deal, both fiction and the other stuff. I did not know what to expect when I began reading Mike's *Speak English* which he had kindly sent me a week ago.

I was hooked after four pages and mesmerized by the 12th. His story, his characters, his understated but poignant allegory kept me reading for hours. I could get specific and cite passages and the like, but I won't. It would be a spoiler. *Speak English* is at once a political heartbreaker and a profound tone poem.

It made me angry, empathetic and wiser for reading it.

Thanks, Mike. Good job.
    ♦ Bob Witkowski

An excellent read...as usual. I was at first put off/confused by the change to your tour narrative in the middle, but it flowed on as you brought it all together. I do like your style. Almost extemporaneous. It reminds me of a story I read long ago of how it took two years to write *A Funny Thing Happened on the Way to the Forum*, which is apparently long for a screenplay, but it shows in that the entertainment itself flows so smoothly that you miss it as it ends.
    ♦ Dan M. Nalven

This book is an amazing blend told with great style of country boy tale-spinning, a road trip across America, conspiracy theories, political manifesto, aliens and flying saucers, and unsparing self-examination. Fascinating from beginning to end as the author tells his story with poetry, humor and wisdom, it is a must-read for all concerned with disappearing democratic values in the U.S. and its catastrophic wars. Read this original, thought-provoking and entertaining book, and learn the truth!
    ♦ Joan Wile is author of *Grandmothers Against the War: Getting Off Our Fannies and Standing Up for Peace*

Mike Palecek is one of this country's best kept secrets. In addition to his heroic activism over the years, Mr. Palecek is a highly talented and accomplished writer whose previous novels I devoured in a single sitting. He's struck gold again with *Speak English*, a book that demands your undivided attention. Dig in!

♦ Jason Leopold, investigative journalist, is author of the Los Angeles Times besteller, *News Junkie*

Mike Palecek is a truly unique, inventive, outrageous, resourceful, funny and exciting writer. We need more like him....and more books like these!!

♦ Harvey Wasserman is author of *SOLARTOPIA* and *HARVEY WASSERMAN'S HISTORY OF THE UNITED STATES*

Evocative writing. Unpredictable tales. A hard political edge. Those are the essential ingredients of Mike Palecek's writing. They're all here in *Speak English*, his best work so far.

♦ Tony Sutton is editor & publisher of ColdType.net and the *ColdType Reader*

Mike Palecek's writing sounds like madness; as complete sanity always does in these insane times. In *Speak English* he once again takes us for a wild ride through a world that's twisted and surreal just enough to be able to speak the simple truth about life inside the sociopathic killing machine we call the Good Ol' U.S. of eff-in' A.

♦ Marc Beaudin is author of *The Moon Cracks Open: A Field Guide to the Birds and Other Poems*, editor of *Jihad Bil Qalam: To Strive by Means of the Pen*, and poetry editor of *CounterPunch*

Speak English poetically weaves together our most urgent, taboo and complex social issues with simplicity, sensitivity and surprising accessibility. Mike brilliantly uses eloquence in the face of tragedy and humor amid horror to bring us a quick-witted and telling tale of depth and connection through the power of the human and not-so-human spirit!

♦ Ava Bird is a poet in Berkeley

If there was a man, one man in a boat and he was gifted, this man, would you share his vision, partake of his hard-earned wisdom if he offered it? He has eyes to see beneath the fishes, separate schools and cloud-rush masses.

This book is the log from his paddle boat, its record a delicate balance of vision and experience, courage and fear, madcap hilarity and frightening actuality, near-misses and direct hits. Hey Mike, I appreciate the opportunity to review this piece. It, you, are a literal pain in the neck. I never read much on the computer screen, too much strain on the ol' eyes, makes my neck and shoulders hurt. I usually print my own stuff off to proofread and edit.

My intention when you sent this was to quick-scan these three hundred or so pages, jot down a blurb and send it to you. I ran into a problem, once begun I couldn't put it down. Now that I've finished it, word for word and page for page, I can't wait to buy a copy to keep me company.

I wanna read it again and again. You got a helluva voice and *Speak English* is a helluva book. Buy it, people. Pick it up and try to put it down before you finish reading it. Good luck with that. I am radical when it comes to authors. After fifty years of reading and writing, there are a handful of them who go down to that deep place, dare to piss me off and lift me up, force me out of my personal box and incite me to think. I've put them on notice to make room for one more. I finished *Speak English*; now I gotta go read all your stuff. Thanks!

> ♦ Tom [WordWulf] Sterner has been extensively published in independent literary magazines and on the Internet. These include Howling Dog Press/Omega, Skyline Literary Review and Flashquake. He is winner of the Marija Cerjak Award for Avant-Garde/Experimental Writing and was nominated for the Pushcart Prize in 2006 and 2008.

The Truth travels.

> ♦ Roy Stokes

Mike Palecek reminds me of Socrates the gadfly who asked unwelcome questions, Diogenes with his lantern looking in vain for an honest man, Chekhov the man with the hammer challenging the complacent family to share their meal, Kerouac the ever on the move, somewhat hysterical searcher, and he reminds me of many Americans who as children were so blasted with propaganda that they're devoting the rest of their lives challenging the lies and all who tell them. In this land where babies are brought by storks and buildings collapse due to unpatriotic bricks, we need the gadfly because no leader, preacher, guru, or saint will wake us up, though the Doomsday clock is ticking close to twelve.

♦ David Ray is author of The *Endless Search*

Mike Palecek's *Speak English* is a book like I like to read.

Crackers and aliens. The crackers are from Iowa. In the American heartland.

I don't think about my troubles for awhile, or the shape the country is in, or things I don't know about, like who caused 9-11, or who killed Senator Wellstone, or was the election — were two elections — really stolen?

Aliens wouldn't be any stranger than the last eight years. In fact, they explain a lot.

Bigfoot, too.

♦ Jack Saunders is author of *Bukowski Never Did This*

Speak English will take you to places you need to go, introduce you to people you need to meet, and invite you to ask questions that perhaps need to be asked.

Bookended between thick, meaty slabs of Mike Palecek's signature staccato, thoughtful and sometimes profane storytelling, the heart of the book traces the author's own bookselling tour from small town Iowa to sophisticated New York. Palecek's theories, including laying responsibility for 9/11 at the gleaming wing-tips of George W. Bush, often play to an unwilling audience, but gift the reader with the best favor an author can give — the urge to think for yourself. Along the way, amid gun-toting teenagers soaked in Clearasil, quart bottles of Schlitz, car windows that refuse to roll down, and the lyrics of Bob Seger or Arlo Gurthrie ringing in one's ears, you may just get the most real taste of the real America on the bookshelf today. As Palecek quotes Steve Earle mid-journey: "The revolution starts now..."

    ♦ Dana Larsen is editor of the Storm Lake Pilot-Tribune

I like Mike, Palecek that is. Why? Because he is a fount of ideas and language, stories, books, websites and provocative commentary intended to ruffle feathers and get us thinking not only about what's wrong — but about what's possible. It is a treat to read his work.

    ♦ Danny Schecter is the News Dissector for MediaChannel.Org

About The Author

Mike Palecek lives in northwest Iowa. He is a former prisoner for peace, congressional candidate, newspaper reporter. He has written several novels.

About the Cover Artist

 ROBERT CARTER is an award-winning illustrator. He was born in St. Albans, England, and moved to Ontario, Canada, at an early age. Robert combines a strong foundation in portraiture with a unique sense of visual and conceptual problem-solving to create striking, vibrant, and textured illustrations and portraits with subjects ranging from the realistic to the surreal. Robert now lives and works as a freelance illustrator in Baden, Ontario, Canada.

About the Publisher

CWG Press is owned and operated by Chuck Gregory in Fort Lauderdale, FL. Rather than limiting our books to a specific genre, we look for books that are of good quality. We choose our authors and our books carefully, and we are proud of them.

ISBN 878-0-9788186-4-7

51495 >

9 780978 818647

www.ingramcontent.com/pod-product-compliance
Lightning Source LLC
Chambersburg PA
CBHW031250170626
46807CB00001B/70